Wyrd and Other Derelictions

Books by
Adam L. G. Nevill

Novels

Banquet for the Damned

Apartment 16

The Ritual

Last Days

House of Small Shadows

No One Gets Out Alive

Lost Girl

Under a Watchful Eye

The Reddening

Cunning Folk

The Vessel

All the Fiends of Hell

Collections

Some Will Not Sleep

Hasty for the Dark

Wyrd and Other Derelictions

Wyrd and Other Derelictions

Adam L. G. Nevill

Ritual Limited
Devon, England
MMXXIII

Wyrd and Other Derelictions

by Adam L. G. Nevill

Published by

Ritual Limited

Devon, England

MMXXIII

www.adamlgnevill.com

Cover design by Simon Nevill

Cover artwork by Samuel Araya

Text design by Peter Marsh

Ritual Limited logo by Moonring Art Design

Printed and bound by Amazon KDP

ISBN 978-1-9163444-4-0

For my 'enabler', Brian J. Showers.

Contents

Hippocampus

Walls of water as slow as lava, black as coal, push the freighter up mountainsides, over frothing peaks and into plunging descents. Across vast, rolling waves the vessel ploughs, ungainly. Conjuring galaxies of bubbles around its passage and in its wake, temporary cosmoses appear for moments in the immensity of onyx water, forged then sucked beneath the hull, or are sacrificed, fizzing, to the freezing night air.

On and on the great steel vessel wallops. Staggering up as if from soiled knees before another nauseating drop into a trough. There is no rest and the ship has no choice but to brace itself, dizzy and near breathless, over and over again, for the next wave.

On board, lighted portholes and square windows offer tiny yellow shapes of reassurance amidst the lightless, roaring ocean that stretches all around and so far below. Reminiscent of a warm home offering a welcome on a winter night, the cabin lights are complemented by the two metal doorways that gape in the rear house of the superstructure. Their spilled light glosses portions of the slick deck.

All of the surfaces on board are steel, painted white. Riveted and welded tight to the deck and each other, the metal cubes of the superstructure are necklaced by yellow rails intended for those who must slip and reel about the flooded decks. Here and there, white ladders rise, and seem by their very presence to evoke a *kang kang kang* sound of feet going up and down quickly.

Small lifeboat cases resembling plastic barrels are fixed at the sides of the upper deck, all of them intact and locked shut. The occasional crane peers out to sea with inappropriate nonchalance, or with the expectation of a purpose that has not come. Up above the distant bridge, from which no faces peer out, the aerials, satellite dishes and navigation masts appear to totter in panic, or to whip their poles, wires and struts from side to side as if engaged in a frantic search of the ever-changing landscape of water below.

The vast steel door of the hold's first hatch is raised and still attached to the crane by chains. This large square section of the hull is filled with white sacks, stacked upon each other in tight columns. Those at the top of the pile are now dark and sopping with rain and seawater. In the centre, scores of the heavy bags have been removed from around a scuffed and dented metal container, painted black. Until its discovery, the container appears to have been deliberately hidden among the tiers of fibre sacks. One side of the double doors at the front of the old container has been jammed open.

Somewhere on deck, a small brass bell clangs a lonesome, undirected cry – a mere nod to tradition, as there are speakers thrusting their silent horns from the metallic walls and masts. But though in better weather the tiny, urgent sound of the bell is occasionally answered by a gull, tonight it is answered by nothing save the black, shrieking chaos of the wind and the water it thrashes.

There is a lane between the freighter's rear house and the crane above the open hatch. A passage unpeopled, wet, and lit by six lights in metal cages. MUSTER STATION: LIFEBOAT 2 is stencilled on the wall in red lettering. Passing through the lane, the noise of the engine intake fans fills the space hotly. Diesel heat creates the impression of being close to moving machine parts. As if functioning as evidence of the ship's purpose and life, and rumbling across every surface like electric current in each part of the vessel, the continuous vibration of the engine's exhaust thrums.

Above the open hatch and beside the lifeboat assembly point, from a door left gaping in the rear house, drifts a thick warmth. Heat that waits to wrap itself round wind-seared cheeks in the way a summer's sun cups faces.

Once across the metal threshold the engine fibrillations deepen as if muted underground. The bronchial roar of the intake fans dulls. Inside, the salty-spittle scour of the night air, and the noxious mechanical odours, are replaced by the scent of old emulsion and the stale chemicals of exhausted air fresheners.

A staircase leads down.

But as above, so below. As on deck, no one walks here. All is still, brightly lit and faintly rumbling with the bass strumming of the exhaust. The communal area appears calm and indifferent to the intense black energies of the hurricane outside.

A long, narrow corridor runs through the rear house. Square lenses in the steel ceiling illuminate the plain passageway. The floor is covered in linoleum, the walls are matt yellow, the doors to the cabins trimmed with wood laminate. Halfway down, two opposing doors hang open before lit rooms.

The first room was intended for recreation, to ease a crew's passage on a long voyage, but no one seeks leisure now. Coloured balls roll across the pool table from the swell that shimmies the ship. Two cues lie amongst the balls and move back and forth like flotsam on the tide. At rest upon the table-tennis table are two worn paddles. The television screen remains as empty and black as the rain-thrashed canopy of sky above the freighter. One of the brown leatherette sofas is split in two places and masking tape suppresses the spongy eruptions of cushion entrails.

Across the corridor, a long bank of washing machines and dryers stand idle in the crew's laundry room. Strung across the ceiling are washing-line cords that loop like skipping ropes from the weight of the clothing that is pegged in rows: jeans, socks, shirts, towels. One basket has been dropped upon the floor and has spilled its contents towards the door.

Up one flight of stairs, an empty bridge. Monitor screens glow green, consoles flicker. One stool lies on its side and the cushioned seat rolls back and forth. A solitary handgun skitters this way and that across the floor. The weapon adds a touch of tension to the otherwise tranquil area of operations, as if a drama has recently passed, been interrupted or even abandoned.

Back down below, further along the crew's communal corridor, the stainless-steel galley glimmers dully in white light. A skein of steam clouds over the work surfaces and condenses on the ceiling above the oven. Two large, unwashed pots have boiled dry upon cooker rings glowing red. From around the oven door, wisps of black smoke puff. Inside the oven a tray of potatoes has baked to carbon and they now resemble the fossils of reptile guano.

Around the great chopping board on the central table lies a scattering of chopped vegetables, cast wide by the freighter's lurches and twists. The ceiling above the work station is railed with steel and festooned with swaying kitchenware.

Six large steaks, encrusted with crushed salt, await the abandoned spatula and the griddle that hisses black and dry. A large refrigerator door, resembling the gate of a bank vault, hangs open to reveal crowded shelves that gleam in ivory light. There is a metal sink the size of a bath tub. Inside it lies a human scalp.

Lopped roughly from the top of a head and left to drain beside the plughole, the gingery mess looks absurdly artificial. But the clod of hair was once plumbed into a circulatory system because the hair is matted dark and wet at the fringes and surrounded by flecks of ochre. The implement that removed the scalp lies upon the draining board: a long knife, the edge serrated for sawing. Above the adjacent work station, at the end of the rack that holds the cook's knives, several items are missing.

Maybe this dripping thing of hair was brought to the sink area from somewhere outside the galley, carried along the corridor from the crew's quarters. Red droplets the size of rose petals make a trail into the first cabin on the communal passage. The door to this cabin is open. Inside, the trail of scarlet is immediately lost within the borders of a far bigger stain.

A fluorescent jacket and cap hang upon a peg just inside the door of the cabin. All is neat and orderly upon the bookshelf, which holds volumes that brush the low white ceiling. A chest of drawers doubles as a desk. The articles on the desktop are held down by a glass paperweight and overlooked by silver-framed photographs of wives and children at the rear of the desk. On top of the wardrobe, life jackets and hardhats are stowed. Two twin beds, arranged close together, are unoccupied. Beneath the bedframes, orange survival suits remain neatly folded and tightly packed.

The bedclothes of the berth on the right-hand side are tidy and undisturbed. But the white top sheet and the yellow blanket of the adjacent berth droop to the linoleum floor like idle sails. There is a suggestion that an occupant departed this bed hurriedly, or was removed swiftly. The bed linen has been yanked from the bed and only remains tucked under the mattress in one corner. A body was also ruined in that bed: the middle of the mattress is blood-sodden and the cabin reeks of salt and rust. Crimson gouts from a bedside frenzy have flecked and speckled the wall beside the bed, and part of the ceiling.

Attached to the room is a small ensuite bathroom that just manages to hold a shower cubicle and small steel sink. The bathroom is pristine; the taps, shower head and towel rail sparkle. All that is amiss is a single slip-on shoe, dropped on the floor just in front of the sink. A foot remains inside the shoe with part of a hairy ankle extending from the uppers.

From the cabin more than a trail of droplets can be followed further down the passage and towards the neighbouring berths. A long, intermittent streak of red has been smeared along the length of the corridor, past the four doors that all hang open and drift back and forth as the ship lists. From each of these cabins, other collections have been made.

What occupants once existed in the crew's quarters appear to have arisen from their beds before stumbling towards the doors as if hearing some cause for alarm nearby. Just before the doorways of their berths, they seem to have met their ends quickly. Wide, lumpy puddles, like spilled stew made with red wine, are splashed across the floors. One crew member sought refuge inside the shower cubicle of the last cabin, because the bathroom door is broken open and the basin of the shower is drenched nearly black from a sudden and conclusive emptying. Livestock hung above the cement of a slaughterhouse and emptied from the throat leaves similar stains.

To the left at the end of the passage, the open door of the captain's cabin is visible. Inside, the sofa beside the coffee table and the two easy chairs sit expectant but empty. The office furniture and shelves reveal no disarray. But set upon the broad desk are three long wooden crates. The tops have been levered off, and the packing straw that was once inside is now littered about the table's surface and the carpeted floor. Mingled with the straw is a plethora of dried flower petals.

Upon a tablecloth spread on the floor before the captain's desk, two small forms have been laid out. They lie side by side. They are the size of five-year-old children and blackened by age, not unlike the preserved forms of ancient peoples, protected behind glass in museums of antiquities. They appear to be shrivelled and contorted. Vestiges of a fibrous binding have fused with their petrified flesh and obscured their arms, if they have such limbs. The two small figures are primarily distinguished by the irregular shape and silhouette of their skulls. Their heads appear oversized, and the swollenness of the crania contributes to the leathery ghastliness of their grimacing faces. The rear of each head is fanned by an incomplete mane of spikes, while the front of each head elongates and protrudes into a snout. The desiccated figures have had their lower limbs bound tightly together to create a suggestion of long and curling tails.

Inside the second crate lies a large black stone, crudely hollowed out in the middle. The dull and chipped appearance of the block also suggests great age. A modern addition has been made, or offered, to the hollow within the stone: a single human foot. The shoe around the disarticulated foot matches the footwear inside the shower cubicle of the first crew member's cabin.

The contents of the third crate have barely been disturbed. In there lie several artefacts that resemble jagged flints, or the surviving blades of old weapons or knives of which the handles are missing. The implements are hand-carved from a stone as black as the basin that has become a receptacle for a human foot.

Pictures of a ship and framed maps have been removed from the widest wall, and upon this wall a marker pen has been used to depict the outlines of two snouted or trumpeting figures that are attached by what appear to be long, entwined tails. The imagery is crude and childlike, but the silhouettes are similar to the embalmed remains laid out upon the tablecloth.

Below the two figures are imprecise sticklike forms that appear to cavort in emulation of the much larger and snouted characters. Set atop some kind of uneven pyramid shape, another group of human characters have been excitedly and messily drawn with spikes protruding from their heads or headdresses. Between the crowned silhouettes another, plainer individual has been held aloft and bleeds from the torso into a waiting receptacle. Detail has been included to indicate that the sacrificed victim's feet have been removed and its legs bound.

The mess of human leavings that led here departs from the captain's cabin and rises up a staircase to the deck above and into an unlit canteen.

Light falls into this room from the corridor, and in the half-light two long tables, and one smaller table for the officers, are revealed. Upon the two larger crew tables long reddish shapes lie glistening: some twelve bodies dwindling into darkness as they stretch away from the door. As if they have been unzipped across the front, what was once inside each of the men has now been gathered and piled upon chairs where the same men once sat and ate. Their feet, some bare, some still inside shoes, have been amputated and are set in a messy pile at the head of the two tables.

The far end of the cafeteria is barely touched by the residual light. Presented to no living audience, perversely and inappropriately and yet in a grimly touching fashion, two misshapen shadows flicker and leap upon the dim wall as if in joyous reunion. They wheel about each other, ferociously, but not without grace. They are attached, it seems, by two long, spiny tails.

Back outside and on deck, it can be seen that the ship continues to meander, dazed with desolation and weariness, perhaps punchdrunk from the shock of what has occurred below deck.

The bow momentarily rises up the small hillside of a wave and, just once, almost expectantly, looks towards the distant harbour to which the vessel has slowly drifted all night since changing its course.

On shore, and across the surrounding basin of treeless land, the lights of a small town are white pinpricks, desperate to be counted in this black storm. Here and there, the harbour lights define the uneven silhouettes of buildings, suggesting stone façades in which glass shimmers to form an unwitting beacon for what exists out here upon these waves.

Oblivious to anything but its own lurching and clanking, the ship rolls on the swell, inexorably drifting on the current that picked up its steel bulk the day before and now slowly propels the hull, though perhaps not as purposelessly as first appeared, towards the shore.

At the prow, having first bound himself tight to the railing with rope, a solitary and unclothed figure nods a bowed head towards the land. The pale flesh of the rotund torso is whipped and occasionally drenched by sea spray, but still bears the ruddy impressions of bestial deeds that were both boisterous and thorough. From navel to sternum, the curious figurehead is blackly open, or has been opened, to the elements. The implement used to carve such crude entrances to the heart is long gone, perhaps dropped from stained and curling fingers into the obsidian whirling and clashing of the monumental ocean far below.

As if to emulate a king, where the scalp has been carved away, a crude series of spikes, fashioned from nails, have been hammered into a pattern resembling a spine or fin across the top of the dead man's skull. Both of his feet are missing and his legs have been bound with twine into a single, gruesome tail.

Wyrd

There are no straight paths here. There is no flat ground.

From on high and looking south, the coastline resembles the great clawed foot of a reptile. Sharp-ridged promontories of shale and volcanic rock, scoured by salt, jut out to rake the sea. Old claws at the culmination of a vast scaly foot, now softened by countless millennia of erosion: the surface made tufty or velveteen with brown gorse and red heather coating the ridges and cuticles.

Between the talons crescent-shaped coves nestle, filled with rubble from old cliff-fall, the greening boulders dull to lead when coated by the sea. Or long stony beaches the colour of iron filings fill the gaps. Inland, where the toes embed into the leviathan's foot, the webbing is fringed by wetland marshes that rise into steep grassy valleys dividing the metatarsals.

If the serrated edge of the land resembles clawed feet, then the rest of the vast beast might be buried beneath the hills: a monumental form sunk deep within dark soil. Inside dripping caverns perhaps the slow, hoarse respiration of the creature's long, deep sleep is detectable and dismissed as air rising through the capillaries of the earth. Perhaps the monster is now of the earth, turned to stone in an ancient, epochal battle, of which vestigial comments exist in ancient poems.

The thin coast path undulates up and down the steep ridges. Occasionally it wanders inland for a stretch before winding and returning to a cliff-edge track. Upon those faint grooves only the nimblest hooves may navigate safe passage above an immensity of empty air. Far below the cliffs, waves the colour of chainmail shatter and spume.

During a journey from the misted distance to here, the land will prove empty of life: no livestock clops the grass flat, no birds shriek about nests in the cliffs, no hares dart or mice flit. An entrant on foot may also experience a sensation of awe as their vision and spirits vault up and into the canopy of empty grey sky. As their eyes sweep north and south they will survey what appears to be an endless range of mountainous promontories breaking the sea in the manner of prows on ships of stone.

This land is wild yet appears barren, is open yet busy with the buffet and slap of unfurling gusts of sea wind. As the kilometres pass beneath tired feet and a traveller ranges up those steep sides on hands and knees, only to endure another difficult descent that screams a protest behind the shinbones, one might even feel uncomfortable: unwelcome in a place seemingly cleansed of living things. Perhaps a traveller is even intimidated by the absence of buildings or phone masts or roads. Passages here are boggy, flinty or slippery by turn and seem eager to urge visitors over edges.

Stray off the path and it is easy to become lost, turned around, bewildered, quickly exhausting oneself within this land's wintry temperament. Maybe one's thoughts are tainted here by this light: an infinite spectrum of grey, from the pale whites of bone and ash near the horizon, to the case-hardened steels and aluminium of the clouds, unrolling in endless sheets that stain the sea a dull pewter.

A lone person is a speck here. A weak form made to sway and totter and stagger amidst the collision of elements. Thoughts are blown about in all directions. Maudlin preoccupations are drawn out by the grey atmosphere. Spend enough time here and a head eventually numbs, its thoughts thinning. In time perhaps there is only an awareness of being diminished, then finally consumed.

Wyrd

After a murderous ascent that flattens the lungs, up a hill distinguished by the crooked silhouettes of black trees that line its summit, there is, finally, some evidence that others have been here before. An occupancy that might bring a surge of optimism to a walker; a heartfelt warmth that accompanies the prospect of companionship in a cold, windswept place.

Below, at the foot of this valley, is a wide ring of brightly coloured tents, their sides soundlessly shivering and rippling in the wind. At the centre of this nylon circle of pup tents, as if they are wagons drawn protectively around an interior space, twelve smaller rings have been neatly formed from pale stones. What lies within the stone circles at such a distance is unclear but the contents are thin and dark-looking. The stone rings suggest fire pits. But why a dozen?

Forming a third ring, an outer ring, and one that is barely visible from up here, are a series of small black lumps. Each tiny mound is set behind a tent. Twelve black lumps, twelve tents, twelve stone circles.

A marsh divides the campsite from the rear of the beach. Still, dark water glimmers in shards like pieces of broken glass between the clumps of the long, blanched grasses. The water is the colour of a beer that might be described as malty, or as having biscuity overtones. Down between the reeds and the highest wavering plumes of the wetland rushes, nothing stirs. Only the tops of the dry stalks gently waver like crowds of tall thin people with wild hair who tiptoe across sharp stones.

The beach is the colour of cold chisels in half-lit workshops. Only sopping wigs of brown seaweed crowning the larger boulders offer any tonal variety. Like a film with all of the green and red removed, the shore has been crushed to a melancholy dimness.

From the wetland and across the rocks, a thin brackish stream moves like a serpent with a disease: a struggling freshwater brook whose unfathomable journey ends here in the foamy surge of the waves, slapping and pawing at low tide. Merely observing this shoreline fills a mind with scent memories: briny shallows, fishy pools of trapped stagnant water, scouring sprays that burn the top of a nose with salt. Old rope. Wet stone. Damp.

The route descending to the beach suggests that steps were once cut into the valley side, but by a blind man of great strength who wielded a pickaxe, his face a grimace, the discoloured marbles of his eyes glimmering with the iron of the sea's surface. And yet these black slippery plates that are embedded in the rock at irregular intervals may also have been formed by landslips of rock that no one heard crash upon the shore below.

Strangely, it also appears that something was once mined here. Opposing each other like empty guard boxes whose sentries have not been on duty for hundreds of years, two lime kilns stand where the rocky shore meets the marsh at either end of the beach. Squat and round, with a small door cut into the front, at a distance the far kiln adds a strange exoticism. It's as if these are remnants of a Stone Age civilisation. The small inner chamber that is visible in the far kiln is blackened with soot. The fire that was lit there is cold, but not so old.

Progress down the steep valley side becomes a hopping and scrabbling over the haphazard arrangement of steps and soon alters the perspective of the valley summit and offers sight of something not apparent when standing at the top: the trees around the entire rim of the valley are precisely spaced apart. They resemble burned men, somehow still upright and in formation, with their raised arms and reaching fingers seared to bone and down to the knuckle. And yet there is also something Grecian about these scarecrow saplings: an ancient order, a system of uprights or columns that mark a boundary, a perimeter.

Nearer the bottom of the valley, when the din of the relentless waves wallops and fizzes, the trees at the summit begin to resemble crows upon a wire, or even distant warriors on horseback poised before the whooping and swooping begin.

The crooked stairway ends upon the sand beside the nearer kiln. And this stone oven, so carefully constructed by stones laid one upon another, now issues tones of the mausoleum. The blackened oval interior more than suggests the crematorium too, because amidst the greasy accumulation of ash, seared bones are visible. Though from what animal they originate is not clear.

Marsh reeds obscure the campsite. One must move up a stony track at one side of the quiet wetland to reach the tents. And in that gulley, as one passes through, there is a rustling as dry brown stalks are stirred by a breeze that probes inwards from the sea. Eventually, the pathway ends as the valley floor opens and reveals the *circles*: the small black lumps, the rippling nylon of the tents, and the stone circles of the interior.

Once closer to the outer ring, these dark lumps take on an unappealing aspect. Half concealed by the long grass, what is visible is partially ruffled by the wind and it soon becomes clear that these *forms* are not made from rock or wood but are of flesh and blood. They are still and stiff and somehow huddled into themselves.

About the first one, blood has drained blackly onto the grass and taken on the appearance of ink but also congealed to resemble drying tar. There is a small hoof extending into the air at the end of a thin black leg and a murky eye soon appears inside a woolly head; an eye the size of an olive but made rheumy by death. The black fleece has caught seeds blown from the plumes of the marsh.

Beneath the infantile head, a dark crimson gash, like a necklace of pulped summer fruits, glistens amidst the surrounding fur. It is a lamb. These are lambs. Black lambs. Slaughtered and arranged in a circle like the symbols on some strange clock, each tufty carcase at the same distance behind a tent.

The tracks of the feet of those who knelt here to destroy the small, defenceless animals are still faintly impressed upon the grass. The trails lead to the spaces between the tents. All around the outer circle, as one treads lightly, the same pattern of trampled grass can be observed, leading from a dead lamb to the circular space inside the ring of tents. The tracks might be the spokes of some giant wheel.

Beside the first tent, itself a daub of blue amidst the dark green of uncut grass, the central stone circles become a regular sequence of indents depressing sections of overgrown grass. Their contents remain hidden. But when this ordinary blue tent or any of the others are opened, their close and colourful interiors will be found empty of life. It is as if these shelters were abandoned in the middle of some expedition by people who observed orderly habits. They left their torches. Their sleeping bags are unfurled upon inflatable beds or foam mats. Rucksacks of various sizes and descriptions lie flat or half empty. No food is visible inside the tents. But before the door of each inner compartment it would be impossible not to notice the piles of neatly folded clothes stacked beside a pair of walking boots. This suggests the occupants removed their footwear and stripped their bodies of every stitch of clothing before taking to their humble beds. And yet these beds are empty, as empty of bodies as the clothes layered in the neat, square piles.

The only other detail repeated within each interior and shielded by the shuddering fabric walls is a specific item. A book. A book that resembles a bible bound in black leather. Each volume in each tent is identical and laid carefully upon the foot of the beds. No author is cited, but in gold leaf each spine displays the title: WYRD. On the front cover, also embossed in gold leaf, is a symbol resembling a rune. A rune that may depict a bird or some kind of winged figure.

Within the circle of empty tents lie the stone rings, and if the rings draw the eye it is because they are constructed from limestone blocks: stone that has been ferried to the grass from somewhere else, or hewn from the hills where the limestone parts the basalts and dolerite, the shale and slates. Limestone must be present nearby because those kilns at the shore, even though they are now filled with charred bones, were designed to process limestone for fertiliser.

But few eyes would linger long upon the twelve neat rings

of pale stone, because of what lies within these circlets. That is far more compelling. If each ring were checked in turn, inside ten of them a body would be found. A naked body, or what remained of such.

The event for which these preparations were made is long past, but this butchery appears to have signalled its climax.

In the centre of ten of the stone rings, the ragged and tortured statements of human forms lie still. But none have been restrained. No bindings or manacles encircle the wrists or ankles, the limbs are free and not pegged to the ground.

Despite the slaughter enacted on this cold grass, two of the forms have even managed to maintain a star shape that must have been assumed when the body was first positioned within the ring, with the arms and legs outstretched, or spread-eagled, as they faced the grey sky. As for the exposed rib cages, black as burned bacon and revealed in the manner of zebra or gazelle slaughtered and scavenged upon the savannahs of Africa, to have stayed in such a position as the torsos and cavities were emptied so thoroughly suggests a shocking commitment.

Eyes, tongues, noses and ears are absent from each of the ten faces at rest within the stone rings. In their place, holes gape blackly. Apart from the extractions, what's left of the faces remains unbroken but coloured red from forehead to chin. Blood doesn't run in smooth planes over curved surfaces, so these faces must have been painted with a scarlet dye or cosmetic prior to death. What remains of the untouched flesh below the heads, the throats and shoulders, is pale where unstained by dried blood. This poses the question: did these pasty, naked figures paint their faces red before they'd entered the rings of stone?

Though ten of the rings contain these much reduced human forms, two are empty. And yet the grass is much disturbed within and around them. This pair of empty stone circlets lie closest to the wetland, and nearby it quickly becomes possible to see what befell the occupants: two bodies lie motionless amongst the reeds at the fringe of the marsh.

Their contorted limbs suggest a terrible struggle before they met their end. And it is tempting to suspect that this pair suffered a change of mind, perhaps whilst a grisly business within the rings of their fellows and neighbours was in process. But these two people either bolted out of their rings or were lifted from them before being dropped onto the wetland's border, because only *their* legs are broken.

Though all twelve of the bodies have been partially flayed, and all have lost the genitals and the muscles from the thighs down to the bone, only the lower legs of the pair lying in the reeds of the wetland are loosened from their hinge joints and pointing out at odd angles from what's left of the knees.

Where hair still remains among the stained scalps of the twelve silent, inert figures, it is white. In four cases, vestiges of curled perms are visible, so these people were elderly. What can still be identified of the hands and feet and arms also attests to the age of the victims.

Given the grisly evidence, a witness would indeed be sickened, but whether the greatest horror here is evoked by how the twelve died, or whether they died voluntarily, remains a matter of individual taste and conscience. But it is rational to assume that a dozen lambs were slaughtered before twelve people carefully undressed inside their tents and made their way to the twelve stone rings. Where they then lay down. And waited.

There is a symmetry here, an order, near perfect save for the two who may have been taken from their rings and butchered in the reeds. Or maybe they arose from a supine position and ran during some hectic final moments (when anyone could be forgiven for attempting to evade this fate), but were soon seized, despatched and field-dressed beyond the stone circlets.

To turn a head at this juncture and to gaze up at the sky – that vast gaseous realm that has been a constant yet featureless canopy to any journey that leads here – may also usher in another perspective and one that is as sudden as it is startling.

It has been written that birds see the earth as a colourless aerial photograph and that they navigate by the shapes and features within the land so far below. So these three rings – the lambs, the tents, the stone circles – are not dissimilar to the markings and signs seen from above in crop fields. They would certainly stand out when viewed from high above in the atmosphere. So was that for whom these circular patterns and rings were intended: something *of the air*? What purpose the cries and blood of the black lambs then? A signal?

Up there, in the swirl and sweep of the layered wisps of grey, none could be blamed for imagining the presence of something keenly sighted that may have long scrutinised this part of the earth. Is there legacy in this remote place? An enduring familiarity with what was recently done here? After all, these circular arrangements of lambs, tents and living bodies within stone rings are only visible from upon the valley's ridge, or from the vast canvas of sky above this receptacle.

One can almost imagine a disturbance in that grey ocean of vapour. Perhaps a parting of the cloud too, followed by a terrible cry. And then the growing of a shadow upon the earth, one great enough to have slowed the blood of anything that found itself upon this ground. The descent must have come at a terrifying velocity unto what had laid itself out, willingly. Or mostly.

Turning the Tide

*I*t is as if no one has arrived.

An empty cove. Hours after sunrise. The vast sea a spectrum of blue tones, cloud-shadowed from dark and forbidding to pale and reassuring beneath clear sky. Calm as a millpond as far as the horizon.

No one sits and looks out. No dogs mad with glee dart into the water. No small children purposefully totter about the rock pools, their plastic buckets swaying. No towels, no sun umbrellas, no beach toys. Only a profound stillness, extending from the surface of the sea to the woods collaring the cove. A quiet moment after an event when time itself pauses for the world to make sense of recent occurrences.

The shoreline between the wood and the water is the crimson of paprika. A gritty surface of ruffled red sand, interspersed with black rocks that regularly break through the undulating peppery grains.

A groove splits the red sand of the beach. Four metres wide, a few centimetres deep. The long furrow extends from the darker sand where small waves swish, then crosses the powdery sun-bleached band the sea never scours. Inside the treeline at the rocky rear of the cove, the ploughed trough vanishes.

Sheltered by the forested hill above, the rear of the cove lies damp with shadow. Larch and sweet birch trees fringe the crescent-shaped beach. Like tired runners who bend forward to clutch their knees, their branches, caped heavy in dark green, overhang black rocks. Dense and lush, the woody canopy extends up the hill and over the cliffs of the limestone peninsulas that extend a protective embrace around each side of the beach.

Air warming yet still pierced by night's subsiding chill. Sluggish air, spiced with salt, the billions of slowly warming granules of sand and the pungent damp issuing from the wet floor of the wood. A blinding sun rises behind the hill and casts the long, twisted shadow-limbs of the trees across the brighter sand.

Sea cormorants and speckled fledgling gulls, only now return to the water with a growing momentum. They appear alert if not self-conscious, regrouping in a place from which they were startled away.

There is little sound save the dry whittle-rattle of the breeze in the nodding, dipping leaves of the wood, and the slop and languorous fizz of gentle waves upon the shore. And yet there has been other activity here, because the cove's sand has recently been divided by this ploughed stripe: a long, unbroken and determined corrugation that extends from the sea and into the trees. The scar is recent. A shallow trench exposing moist sand beneath the powdery crust, the cut not yet blanched by the early sun's growing warmth.

A new sound. Sudden. Piercing. Incongruous in this still-life momentarily devoid of human congress.

Music. Pinging electronic music. A phone's ringtone.

Some way between the shoreline and the visor of drooping trees, a phone lies upon the sand, its rectangular screen suddenly alight with the green icon of a telephone. A word announces the caller: *Police*. This instruction flashes for six seconds.

Moments expire and the screen dims. Then, coinciding with an electronic chime, it is lit up again, this time by a thin white banner that announces: *You have been left a message from Police*. The time is given: 10:15am.

As if the device is eager to return to deep sleep, the lights on the screen dissolve to a black, glassy void. Any sound is sucked back inside the handset.

This phone and two other handsets that become visible in the sand lie outside the four-metre-wide furrow, as if they were dropped over the side of whatever made the track in the red sand. One device is depressed into the ground and the screen shows the wintry veins of cracked ice. Despite the damage inflicted upon the handset, the item functions and beneath the web of shattered screen a light soundlessly flashes orange. The text is just visible beneath the shattered screen. *Mum. Mum* is calling someone called *Kayleigh*, to whom the phone must belong.

Other colourful objects become noticeable against the sand that is dark red, the colour of old meat, where it is nudged by small waves. The objects have also been placed or dropped beside the groove in the sand, or depressed into the long furrow.

A child's toy, a pink giraffe with purple spots, marks itself out, the ruddy granules clinging to its artificial fur like a disease. One black and amber eye is encrusted with sand as if shelled by a painful cataract. The second eye stares blankly, straight up, at the empty blue sky. Thus abandoned and soiled with sand, the giraffe's expression suggests a swift alteration from intended cuteness to mute shock.

Inside the track carven into the beach's surface, long drag marks mirror the patterns of outstretched hands, as if fingers have tried to cling to a loose surface to slow a passage to or from the sea, or to or from the fringe of woods.

Closer, the trunks and branches of the trees are white where they are visible betwixt a rigging of bright ivy that pythons each trunk. In one discreet aperture at the wood's hem, the trees arch over a narrow tarmac track unsuitable for vehicles. A metal handrail made from scaffolding poles is cemented at one side of the path, the upper surface of the tubes purpled from years of use.

Up through the valley of trees covering the red soil of the hill, the tarmac ribbon of footpath curves towards a disc of thin air, brilliant with sunlight: a clearing within the canopy of trees that suggests a celestial destination.

At various junctures on this shaded path, the surface glistens like the tar is freshly poured. A dark, viscous liquid has spattered and been smeared by whatever was dragged across the stains. Small flies gather about the wet streaks as if about dark treacle slopped upon a kitchen floor.

Passing out of the shaded, forested tunnel encroaching upon the path, and entering this silvery light, the briny tang of the seashore's air and the muffled sweet rot of the wood's root-veined floor is replaced. The fragrance of newly cut grass within a great vault of open, clear air braces an ascent from the cove below.

Close-cropped grass, the colour of freshly shelled peas, broadens into a wide and almost treeless paddock. Only a few oaks have clung on, their gnarly, muscular shins black as pitch against the long, bright lawn. Around the trees at the far end of the paddock, as if huddled for companionship, or to share an umbrella against a summer shower of rain, stand five tents. They are tethered to the ground where the paddock ends and the distant rows of white static caravans resemble immaculate tombs in a well-groomed cemetery.

Below the five erect tents visible on the wide plain of tended grass, many other tents have collapsed like parachutes that have wafted to earth. Great colourful bags of artificial fabric, the colourful panels stretched out and lying flat; in places they are bulbous where their disordered contents bulge. The position and shape of the collapsed tents suggest that they have been pulled like heavy sacks along the grass from where the disinterred, dark iron tent pegs lie uprooted and bent out of shape.

Forming a perimeter before the treeline at the foot of the grassy paddock containing the tent plots, a single line of silver and white camper vans is arranged in a neat row. They hug the border of the wood like an additional defence or second wall. An empty vehicle is parked beside all but one of the motor-homes. Around some of the caravan doors, candy-striped windbreaks with wooden uprights form an additional corral of privacy for the occupants.

All of the doors of the camper vans are as open and dark as mouths widened in surprise.

One all-terrain vehicle appears to have been driven forward from the motor-home's designated cement parking rectangle before being abandoned about twenty metres from the parking space. All four doors hang open; one seatbelt loops from the rear and touches the grass.

Turn around.

Close to the nearest tent, a reminder of the campsite's proximity to the sea is visible on the neat, shorn grass. Near translucent and still glimmering with salt water, long bands of brown weed stretch across the earth. Thongweed that has not been strewn here long enough to dry crispy and shrivel into brittle twigs, exposed to the sun and air. Tangled about itself, pooling where the tent's zippered door was torn away, the great glistening spaghetti of seaweed is fresh and brown.

Wet and creased, the white netting of the tent's inner lining and the blue nylon of a porch canopy lie discarded like wet rags upon the grass. This portion of the tent has been tugged out from the collapsed mess, a boneless wing. Glossy, tough and viscous, strands of wet thongweed disappear inside the demolished tent as if burrowing for survivors.

An odour lingers. A fading fragrance of supple marine life; a thin, oily perfume that penetrates the sinuses whenever a nose passes over the silvery flanks of a large fish to assess its freshness. A glance at each of the collapsed tents reveals the same lengths of coiled or probing thongweed about the broken canopies. Each ruin is misted by the spore of fish skin sparkling and dripping with the sea's diamonds.

Beside the collapsed and strewn wreckage of a family tent, another strident scent mingles with the taint of wet scales and dew-moistened grass. An odour of wet dog fur hangs in an invisible cloud about the ugly tears in the tent's bright panels. A smell that grows more pungent with proximity and is soon spiced with the ammonia of exposed kidneys and sun-warmed offal.

The body of the lifeless dog becomes visible.

The animal is stretched out beside the red car that neighbours the tent. One hooded eye is already being explored by flies. A purple tongue extends between bared teeth and hangs from the mouth as if attempting to escape the violence inflicted upon the dog's body.

Between the animal's stiff legs, the pale underside of its belly has been reduced in the manner of the flattened tents, the capacity and volume squashed flat or removed. Purple and oyster-coloured organs, shaped like plastic bags amidst the wormlike vessels of a digestive system, extend from the dog's belly in a foul curtain that stains the grass black. Though it was once an overweight Golden Retriever, so large was the bite that took the dog's flank back to the spine that the animal's dark silhouette has been transformed to that of a spindly greyhound.

No occupants remain inside the collapsed tents. But the rucksacks, bedding, boxes of food, personal effects and camping equipment have been left behind. All rolled together and mingled as the tents became bags that were tugged across the grass. Some items have spilled from the rents made in the fabric panels, as access was sought to whatever struggled inside these brightly coloured sacks.

The five tents of various styles and sizes that remain upright at the top of the field, ranging from a one-man tent to something that might have contained a small circus, were evacuated hurriedly. The interiors reveal sleeping bags cast open like drunken mouths, or tangled amidst collapsible tables and chairs subjected to their own sudden rearrangements. In one tent an airbed has been punctured flat and is streaked crimson. This suggests that while the tents closer to the treeline were seized and dragged along the grass and then emptied of their living contents, the sleepers in the still erect tents had some time, perhaps only moments, to arise and unzip their doors. And to look out at whatever commotion had disturbed them.

Some of the occupants of the tents that have remained whole may have made off on foot. Each upright tent is still shielded on one side by the owner's parked vehicle, so no one left this campsite in a car. In one case, two mountain bikes remain chained to each other like inseparable lovers.

But the evidence also suggests that the occupants of the erect tents never escaped this paddock. They were instead surprised and unable to range much further than their hastily unzipped doors, those thin fabric shields that covered their sleeping compartments. Not far from the gaping doors, items of night clothing lie discarded upon the grass. Here and there a T-shirt litters the neat, even surface of the green paddock. A towelling dressing gown is splayed, the empty arms thrust out wide as if to signal for rescue from above. Several pairs of rubber flip-flops mark the grass near three of the upright tents. But they do not lie alongside each other. A distance as great as twenty metres could be measured between each rubber shoe belonging to the same pair, as if one flip-flop left a foot *here* and the second slipped off the other foot *there*.

Three more phones are visible against the grass, their screens blank and dark.

A single sleeping bag, lying some distance from the upright tents, has been pulled inside out, top to bottom. Flattened grass, forming a chute behind the sleeping bag, indicates how the bedding was tugged from an erect tent and dragged across the grass for some distance, the weight of the occupant inside the sleeping bag smoothing an ominous track across the field. The white fleece lining of the bag is stained as if the sleeper's bowels gave out at some point during their transport across the neatly shorn paddock. The damp stain is investigated by flies.

All of the detritus suggests the intended destination of whoever slept inside the tents, whether erect or collapsed. The messy smear of discarded clothes, shoes and belongings leads to the tarmac path connecting the campsite to the cove of furrowed red sand that lies below.

Enlivened

*B*efore us, a rock. About us, darkness.

Aged limestone dimly lit from below. A dolmen, pale in patches on its raised features but mostly weathered green, blotched like verdigris on copperplate. A pillar stained the tinge of dried mucus or dead seaweed; a palette of nausea when observed for more than moments. A monolith of stone pored and burrowed by creatures no longer infesting the rock; the uneven surface pockmarked with sinuses, tiny tunnels that end in black. Honeycombed from the myriad of tiny mouths that chewed stone during a vast swathe of time in the sea, or perhaps a cave where it patiently awaited excavation.

A rough design is inscribed on the front of the menhir. Unsavoury form emerges upon this crude column that stands within an iron caliper, rooted to the floorboards. Is that a bulbous abdomen fashioned by Neolithic hands, from a time of frost and tundra, wild times without words? Are they wings, foetal and insubstantial, that cling to the sides of the rock? Was this a likeness, or an impression, wrought by an artist, or priest? And what does the faint, ghastly image depict? Can we assume that the pointed or beaked shape crowning this lumpen bas-relief was once a fearsome head tilted to shriek? Is this an ancient royal crest hewn into rock? Or an image of something once worshipped? A symbol? A territorial marker? Was it brought here from a lonely vigil in a misted, wet landscape, or from the ruins of a temple? The rock's carving conjures all such purposes and settings.

From its cold breast an aroma wafts and lingers in heavy air. An ecclesiastical flavour, mingling with the mineral scent of damp stone. Something has been sprinkled, consecrating the crude rock. Frankincense, a sweet piney resin. Vetiver, a twist of citron. And something more pungent, like almonds, adorns, honours and respects this stone.

About the foundations of the pillar, a myriad tealight candles glimmer in the last of the liquefied wax upon which they float like small yellow hands waving from tiny grey seas. Close to extinction, the dimming candlelight ripples the engulfing dark and the silent, hallowed air that surrounds the rock.

Two bowls sit at the foot of the column. Simple, unadorned wooden containers.

The contents of the first bowl glimmer the black of treacle or fresh oil. A tidemark, the red of beets, is visible above the slippery onyx surface of the liquid.

In the second bowl, two egg-shapes slump together. Soft and dull, partially squashed or collapsed: eyes. And now that sight has left the pair of discarded orbs inside the bowl, the sclera has tarnished an unhealthy grey and the irises have misted and been sheathed with a pellucid veil. These sticky misshapen lumps were once blue eyes. There is still a trace of a dark sea where they bulge at the front and a vague sheen persists about the dead flesh, mere memory of the lustre these eyes once possessed when alive and blinking and seeing and rotating within a human face.

About the rock, the bowl of blood, the bowl of eyes, and the many candles whose flames shrink to feeble points the size of match-heads, the dark oppresses. This space, this sanctum, is tuned to a frequency of the deepest silence. The profound stillness creates an uncomfortable pressure as if the space has been lowered into an unseen water that slops beyond the encroaching walls of darkness. The narrowing space about the rock is the last portion of dimming illumination within a mute void that laps at the room and flows from the ceiling. A place smothered by an uncanny quiescence.

Two steps back and withdraw across spiky patterns: lines and angles mark the wooden floor, carefully fashioned from strips of black electrician's tape. Within the shapes marked out by the black lines, messy symbols, curved or jagged, have been fashioned from blood that crusts. An arrangement that indicates an established practice, a rite, a procedure that has been repeated many times in this space.

Against the murky floor, a new shape takes form within the darkness. A body curled into itself. A wretched, uneven, glistening silhouette, its face black with blood. Sunken to inky pulps, the eye sockets gape. From scalp to heel the figure has been peeled and thinned, is wetly gelid.

Wrists bound with green twine, dark fingers knot beneath a glossy chin in supplication. The figure prays. Perhaps for mercy, even now the possibility of reprieve is gone. Thin ankles are tethered like a hen in the window of a restaurant; long feet swell blue below the pinch of their bindings.

The gender is impossible to discern but the figure on the floor was dispatched by the leather thong entwined about their neck. A throttling string knotted about a piece of wood toggles the victim's nape. Strangled. As the wood was turned the leather tightened. Before the votive candles, before the bowls, before the rock, before the dark, they choked.

Further back from the dolmen and the lifeless and stripped body before it, a perimeter marked out by another four candles: one positioned to the front of the dolmen, one behind, one at either side of it, equidistant apart. Thick vanilla candles are mounted on iron stands, still lit but with recalcitrant flames that do little to beat back a darkness near solid.

Four candles that stand before four arches. Apertures appearing as pale eclipses, their dim curvatures positioned at the four points of a compass, the monolith occupying the centre where invisible lines would cross between the arches. A room offering a quartet of opposing entrances, or exits.

Beyond each arched portal little to nothing is visible save more of the dark.

Closer to the first arch, it is possible to see that the empty frame is made of wood, painted black. This door faces south. The floor beneath this oval void feels unstable. An unpleasant vibration runs below the wooden floorboards, one strong enough to interfere with the heart's rhythm, the mind's ability to form thoughts, the respiratory system's essential inhalations and exhalations.

Step away.

To the east.

Where it is not possible to pass from the sanctum and its smothering darkness, or the clinging pall of almonds, frankincense and vetiver. From the blank depth beyond this door, a muscular force of moving air funnels inwards like a bloated river's mightiest current. A hot wind belches from a region as sun-blanched as the hottest desert on earth.

To the west.

Where something worse than wind or the thrumming of an unstable energy exists. Beyond the depthless oblivion of the third portal comes the distant noise of a great beast, sniffing. Too easy to imagine a large muzzle lapping across a floor beyond the aperture; a form wary of entry, but reluctant to retreat.

North.

The northern arch reeks of sulphur. From the centre of the arch, water drips and splashes in minute, invisible explosions, barely discernible slaps against sodden wood.

Beyond the arch, an object glimmers in what light struggles to reach here from beyond this room. A wooden floor can be seen to extend along a narrow passage to the foot of a staircase, the walls on either side impossible to see in any detail. At the summit of the wooden stairs, a dirty yellow light settles.

The object upon the floor of the narrow passage is a scabbard for a sword. The unsheathed sword is not visible, but hard brown leather once gripped the absent blade, the hide now brittle and flaking with age. Brass fittings glimmer where they rib the scabbard, cold to the touch.

Along the passage and up the stairs to an obstacle. A second body.

An old man, his thin face stiffened into a scream that left his mouth in the lightless past of this place; his lips are peeled back from bony gums, fossilised to a rictus. A grimace missing any augmentation from the eyes, which are missing. Empty black wells leer up at the dark from beneath a pale scalp freckled like eggshell. What hair exists at the back and sides of the skull is in wispy disarray. Nostrils ungroomed, eyebrows tangled like wires at the end of a severed cable. A head that has turned too far backwards. The figure might have been looking over its shoulder before the whole head became unmoored at the furthest extent of the intended rotation.

His clothing is ordinary: a woollen cardigan, bottle-green corduroy trousers, belted tight, maroon socks on shrivelled ankles, innocuous black shoes, still laced. But the man's slight and pointed frame appears flatter than it should, as if his body has been pressed into the stairs. The figure may have been stepped upon. A closer scrutiny of the clothing also suggests a lumpiness caused by the breaking of the body inside the surrounding, confining fabric, so that the garments now function as bags to hold the limbs and trunk together.

The steel of a ceremonial sword lies two steps above one outstretched and frail hand, the polished blade a dull smear in thin light.

At the summit of the staircase, an open door.

Electric light glows within a hallway beyond the door, tainted the hue of a faded photograph.

A pall of stale air reeking of almonds is trapped behind the curtained windows of the ground floor. A closeness further compressed by drab wallpaper and yellowing ceilings.

On the far left of the reception, a cluttered kitchen, its fittings and fixtures not modernised in decades. Once white doors of cabinets and drawers sallowed by sunlight and cooking stains. Orange lino worn to ivory by decades of feet shuffling between aged, enamelled appliances, whose surfaces are a murder scene of baked grease and spills transformed from liquid to solid.

Fragile wooden blinds, their ties impenetrable knots bunching like fibrous grapes, shut out most of the light, leaving a little glaring from the corners of the window frames.

Across the counter tops a spiky battlefield of unwashed crockery and murky containers. The tins and jars with their congealed contents are like beakers in an abandoned laboratory. A toaster is pressed into the wall, blackened as a car-wreck. Breadbin: its door kicked in. A coloured tongue of unwashed clothes pours onto the floor from the washing machine's porthole.

A third body. Jammed into the corner of the kitchen.

Beside the metal sink that grows a tower of stained bowls and rimed pans, and amidst a scaffolding of begrimed utensils, part of a woman is visible. From the waist upwards, she has disappeared inside the confines of a cupboard between the cooker and sink. The door of the wooden unit has been smashed inwards from the force of her entry. Fresh splinters of timber spike from the frame around buckled hinges. A pair of fat legs inside taut taupe slacks jut into the room. White socks cover thick ankles. Cream shoes fastened with a velcro strap conceal oddly small feet that look silly despite the shock of their owner being thrust through the door of a kitchen unit.

Beside the legs and portion of abdomen not crammed inside the fitted cupboard lies a small, round shield. The kind of artefact seen in museums of antiquity. It is fashioned from leather stretched across wood, with a wheel-shaped rim and spherical boss of highly polished brass. A shield ceremonial and untested in battle, perhaps until now, but its incongruity amidst the domestic rubble of a messy and unhygienic household is as striking as the discarded sword and scabbard in the cellar: old weapons that offered scant protection against the kind of force that smote these bodies.

A noise from further down the hallway. A sign of life.

From that sound of exertion, it would be easy to imagine that a new-born foal or calf was struggling to get onto spindly legs; hooves skittering in amniotic fluid splashed about a sordid barn; the swollen walnuts of knee-joints banging about a hollow floor. A scrabbling. Then a knocking of hard feet on the hall floor before *it* moves up thinly carpeted stairs.

We are not alone in here. Whatever was just outside has gone upstairs.

From the open doorway of the kitchen, the locked rear of a front door is visible, the fanlight blacked out with messily cut cardboard, sealed in place by black electrician's tape. One panel of cardboard displays the brand of a dog food, stamped in black ink.

The dull, brownish corridor that reeks of frankincense tunnels away, like a pipe-smoker's throat, to a pair of dim rooms on the ground floor.

A glance into the next room on the ground floor. A few patches of red carpet remain visible beneath what looks like earthquake damage. On the floor, what isn't obscured is salted with lint and wormed with ribbons of grey dust. The two lumps might be chairs, but so blanketed are they by rubbish that not even their style nor the patterns of their upholstery are discoverable. Old papers, clothes, cardboard boxes, plastic crates, sloping tiers of books, their covers concealed by poor light, cover the sitting room's furniture, save the top shelf of a cream-coloured bookcase that stands against the far wall, swamped and intimidated.

On the opposite side of this room, the landfill of twisted and neglected belongings reaches to head-height where old Christmas cards, bleached by time, hang on a red string affixed to the dreary floral wallpaper by brass drawing pins.

The door of the neighbouring room lies flat against the floor inside the living room. It has been torn down. The rents in the doorframe, where a hinge was tugged right out of the wood, are fresh.

This room is beset by a shut-in's gloom. Blackout curtains conceal the windows and patio doors. A small lamp on a pile of newspapers casts an undersea glow over a table. Meals were eaten upon it, but the crockery was never cleared. At least a dozen mugs, the insides stained by tannin to the colour of unclean mouths, litter the surface. Dark tidemarks of grime tapestry the odd-coloured ceramic bowls; stale toast turned to wood rests in a galaxy of black crumbs. An open packet of shortbread biscuits slouches atop magazines and puzzle books.

Beside an easy chair, its cream and rose fabric darkened by the grease of use and spills, a cloth bag is open like a sloppy drunk's mouth from which wool and knitting paraphernalia spill.

Between the gas fire and the messy table, the fourth body.

A woman, face-down on a dirty red rug before the fire's grate. A shock of white hair, cotton-wool-wild on one side but matted wet and dark on the other. Her legs shoot out at angles impossible to effect within the ball-and-socket joints of a human pelvis. One slip-on shoe has left a foot. Her arms reach out, in line with her narrow back, like a skydiver's. One hand still clutches a wooden cup shaped like a goblet, its style suggesting it was made centuries ago. Nothing spills from the cup.

The rest of the room's furnishings and artefacts are mundane, ordinary, in disarray, lazily cast down and never picked up again. Except for the picture above the mantel. A large oil, the palette so sombre it is difficult to determine the subject of the portrait, save that something the colour of shadow wears a crown and spreads murky wings.

Incongruously, despite the meagreness, dirt and orderless nature of this home, the frame of the painting is coated in a lavish gold-leaf and moulded like an extravagant cornice. Within the frame, scores of small, naked human figures are depicted. They entwine as if climbing over each other.

Back down the tobacco-stained chute of the hallway to the staircase. Almonds. Vetiver. Frankincense.

Silence upstairs, the stairwell as close and murky as a grimy maw opened to yawn behind the bars of a zoo.

First floor: four closed doors. Upon the landing, a dull thump, muted through the ceiling. Followed by the scraping of a substantial weight along a carpeted floor. When the dragging noise ceases, as if the process has been abandoned, hard feet scatter across the floorboards. A door is slammed shut further along the landing, towards the front of the property.

We are not alone here.

Up the stairs to the next storey of a grim building that remains in permanent night, as if the rising of each new dawn was an insult to whatever morbid preoccupations gripped the sleepers, residents or guests, who woke here each day until their last.

Four doors, all thickly painted a red so dark that it appears brown in what dismal light wafts up the stairwell. Three of the doors are shut. One doorway gapes, the door hanging from a single hinge, the upper hinge smashed free of the timber. The master bedroom.

Looking inside the master bedroom from the landing, what sunlight strains through thin yellowy curtains casts a malarial sheen over a murky space crowded with furniture. A vast unkempt bed the centrepiece. Shabby bedclothes, tangled and hopelessly creased, hang from the divan's side and rear. The floor at its side a veritable swamp of discarded garments, newspapers, books, crockery.

From the doorway of this immediately accessible room, two large wardrobes become visible, as dark and cumbersome as upright coffins, filling the two gloomy far corners like sentries unwilling to be seen and unlikely to issue challenges. At the foot of the bed, forming an antique bridge between the two wardrobes, a chest of drawers or dresser. It's hard to imagine being able to pass between the end of the bed and this article of furniture if its drawers were left open. Atop the dresser, running its entire length, a silvery rectangle of mirror reflects the opposite side of the room: tangled bedclothes upon the unhealthy bed become visible, grey pillows indented with the shape of a head, two bedside cabinets, their surfaces step-pyramids of medication packets and empty cups atop books and discarded tissues. A pair of reading glasses peers at a dim ceiling.

A few steps inside the room and the feet of the fifth body become visible, trapped between the end of the bed and the dresser. Ordinary black shoes, schoolish in appearance, are neatly laced up beneath the turnups of a pair of grey trousers.

A glance into the shadowy trench between bed and dresser reveals a thin, elderly male body lying on its back. Each arm is still partly raised, as if flung outwards at the last moment. The fingers of one hand still grip the brass handle of a dresser drawer; the other hand and wrist remain coiled within the bedclothes, presumably fisted as the victim faced the violence of the attack that left him lifeless. Perhaps he clutched the sides of the ravine to prevent himself being dragged out.

Sticking upwards, like an antenna or aerial, a thin wooden stick protrudes from the hand lost within the bed sheets. The wooden stick, or wand, was gripped until the last moment. A close and knowledgeable scrutiny would identify the wood as oak.

Above the extended arms, the head resembles smashed pottery partly held together by a pale-coloured sack. As the body was pulled along the floor from where it was dispatched, and perhaps from beneath the bed where the man had been hiding, the top of the head has smeared away into the darkness. The stain spreads into discarded clothing and the pages of a broadsheet, the paper called upon to demonstrate the absorbent properties of newsprint. The lower jaw of the face is intact, though a pair of detached false teeth seem to form a second mouth within the one stretched so unnaturally wide.

A door clicks open.

Outside the room, somewhere on the dim landing, cumbersome feet bump, scrabble and kick like a panicked animal compelled from its pen. The pervasive smell that has lingered inside the building intensifies. Heavy and sickly, a tinge of almonds amidst a new perfume of tropical flowers and sweet rot, spills across the landing and into the dim master bedroom.

Moments after the hard, stamping feet become audible on the landing outside, the mirror of the dresser at the end of the unkempt bed where the broken man is wedged is busy with motion. Framed within the rectangle of the doorway but partly obscured by the tilting door, a brief moment of revelation is granted. The aperture darkens, is filled.

A flash of torso beneath embryonic wings, raised as if for a fledgling's first flight. Long ribs as if glimpsed through a tadpole's abdomen. What functions for a head is intricately boned, the beak stained, not unlike that of a great plucked bird. A crown of wood upon the ghastly skull.

What lopes across the open doorway of the master bedroom is soon gone, crossing the landing to reach the staircase in a single stride. Then it vanishes from sight, the rickety legs and long toes carrying it away and down.

A skittering of sharp, heavy feet from below in the hall.

A thumping of an ungainly body through the aperture of the cellar door.

A far-off scratching of claws on bare wooden steps, diminishing, descending. Gone.

Silence.

Almonds. Vetiver. Frankincense.

Monument

To know why it was there, you would first need to know that it was there. Had someone known that it was there before now, theories would have abounded about who built it, and why, and for what or whom it was constructed. But there is no signage and the passage appears to have only recently been discovered.

At present, daylight has not long fallen through a small entrance perhaps closed for millennia, bronzing the interior, partially uncovering this space beneath the earth. Natural light extends a pale band that soon degrades into a vague, powdery illumination, cast across the stone floor in the rectangular shape of the trilithon entrance: a small doorway no more than a metre high, constructed from three stone slabs, two vertical and one horizontal, the latter laid perfectly across the two upright columns.

To enter the chamber within the hill, you must first sink to the earth and move forward and into the darkness on hands and knees, passing under the stone lintel; through a crawlspace into what might be a long barrow, or a causeway, perhaps a cursus, or possibly a tomb-shrine or passage-grave. Some of the soil packed into the opening passage has collapsed inside the hollow centre of the mound which opens around the block of dim light.

From the diminutive entrance, a central avenue of stone extends until the darkness resumes a smothering hold. A natural refrigeration of soil and stone shivers the skin.

Mineral scents of wet earth and rock, moistened by seepage, monopolise the senses. After initial moments of adjusting eyesight to the gloom of the subterranean space, more of the chamber's construction can be observed.

Blocks of bluestone artfully form the walls of a circular chamber. The low ceiling is fashioned from long stone lintels and decomposing lengths of wood braced against the weight of earth above.

Immediately to the left, a circular pit sinks into the floor: a bowl-shaped cavity lined with sandstone blocks worked with precise joinery. Articles of flint glimmer amidst a bed of soil, the colour of black tea, that has fallen from the low ceiling. Once cleaned with the tail of a shirt, a variety of near pristine arrow-heads and axe-heads can be appreciated. Here are beads too, made from iron, carefully worked and bored. And here, an intact weaving comb carved from bone.

A little deeper inside, more grave goods become apparent in a second circular pit. These contents are less obscured by roof-fall. A mosaic of potsherds manufactured from a variety of coloured clay litters the bowl. Fired expertly, the colours have barely faded.

Going further. Rising from hands and knees, a crouch is possible but one must move sideways, head dipped to evade the hard ceiling. Hard lumps now roll beneath hands and feet in a sliding motion reminiscent of loose gravel or pebbles beneath palms and soles. Across the flagstone floor, in places less obscured by the soil that has trickled or slumped inside this cavity beneath the earth, the fainter light reveals evidence of these other artefacts.

Hundreds, if not thousands, of small black lumps, and what appear to be thin, blackened branches, litter the floor-space between and beyond the circular pits rimmed by smoothed sandstone. A great casting and scattering of charcoal-tinted lumps spreads until the light vanishes inside the chamber below the ground.

A quick inspection of the nearest fragments and it will become apparent that these lumps are pieces of bone.

Longer pieces prove hollow inside. Others are still honeycombed by petrified blood vessels and marrow. Textures vary, from crumbling to firm, but all are feather-light and a pale willow to coal-black in hue. Under scrutiny, some of the articles emerge as intact ribs and vertebrae, metatarsals and knuckles. Cindered remains that must have been interred here. Depositions, because the bluestone walls are not singed and layered with soot like the walls of old crematoria; they remain pale and moist. Burned animal bones were brought here, gathered here and placed close to something of importance. Perhaps.

Further into the silent darkness, just before the area where daylight fades to a conclusion as ominous as an edge above an unfathomable drop, a third pit makes itself available for inspection. Similar to its counterparts, this hole is sunk through the solid floor. More bones reside. A prickly jumble, a discoloured thicket of spike and filigree. These too must be ceremonial depositions and they offer a greater mystery, because these bones differ in size and appearance from those scattered about the floor. These remains once belonged to birds. Amidst the rubble of so many collapsed skeletal constructions, small breastplates curve and splinter amidst shafts as thin as pins and skulls so fragile they resemble the shells that once birthed these creatures. Some of these age-browned sticks must have belonged to larger birds, perhaps the bigger corvids.

Back towards the small rectangular passage through which we entered. The light is dimming because the sun is incrementally arcing across the sky, while clouds drift between the sun's rays and the tiny stone-framed aperture of the entrance. A more thorough examination of this intriguing space will be impossible without electric light.

Crawling back across the cramped chamber, a better view is offered of the inner surface of the bluestone walls flanking the entrance. They bear symbols, or designs. Markings not etched by natural subterranean processes. A spiral here. Not perfect yet crudely affecting. Above it, a keyhole shape chipped into the stone. Circles: three, no, four circles resembling small targets, the centre chipped deeper than the two orbiting rings. The meanings of these symbols are not apparent, may be entirely lost. But the patterns must have been left behind by those who returned so many burned bones and silent birds to this sacred space beneath the grassy hill.

A waft of cooler, fresher air, brushes your face. Air that moves and contains within it the scent of grass, thick pollen and a trace of smoke. Air that beckons, filled with the potential of a welcome withdrawal from the ground and a return to daylight.

Squeezing beneath the lintel and the solid door jambs, a momentarily blindness scolds from the intense, white sunlight as clumsy progress is made out of the cold darkness of a distant past: crossing a threshold, between the world of the dead and the belt of the living. Outside again. A return towards open air, a great vault of sky, the din of excited bird calls. Companion calls. A foreign tongue of the heavens heralding a baffling avian celebration.

At the foot of the small grassy mound, branches from the great yew tree that grows nearby cascade and circle the hillock protectively, like an arachnid covering a diaphanous sack of precious, freshly laid eggs. Gnarled, elephant-skinned and warped by the ponderous weight of the great limbs that extend from the papery bark of the trunk, the tree plants its branches like feet astride the mound, all around the circumference of the man-made hill. Leafage casts an additional layer of cover, a shaded canopy to preserve the hill-tomb's silent darkness, a quietude thickening about so many bones.

Facing south, what little is left of the old English wood cowers back from the great red wound that has been cut through the earth. A rent that extends from the mound and the yew to a distant white house, bearded by beds of intensely coloured flowers and a lawn as green and flat as the baize of a snooker table.

Amidst uprooted tree stumps and the tentacles of protruding root systems, a great rectangle has been excavated.

A gash clawed and scraped from the earth by the small red digger that currently stands unmanned and idle.

Within the crater, the edges of a vast gravel bed, recently laid, peek out. Impressed upon the gravel, a neat underslab of poured cement, over which the galvanised steel of rebar reinforcement imprints a skeletal waffle shape. Stacks of grey building blocks, blue pool coping and white tiles wrapped in polythene await their inclusion in the creation of a large swimming pool.

Foundations for a pool gouged out of the old wood. The furthest edge of the excavation clips the sloping skirts of the grassy mound. Once the trees were felled and the undergrowth cleared, the mound presented itself and the ancient yew looked on, naked and fearful and disrobed by the disintegrating perimeter of wood that had concealed and protected what was once a small woodland glade.

Labours and exertions to produce the luxurious swimming pool have paused. No one works in the pit this fine morning. Had men toiled about the great rent in the earth, the cacophony of whistles and caws and shrieks from the receding, battered treeline might have competed with the grind and whine of their power tools and the diesel grunting of plant machinery.

This is a morning unsuited to hard physical labour. The sunlight might have been turned up to cast such a golden cloud upon the garden, the gleaming country house that stands sentinel upon neat hems of patio stone, and the frill of a conservatory. A misted veil of light catches every tree blossom and hollows out bewitching caverns between bordering shrubs where spaces gape. Strange light falls here and douses the mulchy flower beds, inciting riots of pastel. A garden made impressionistic by shimmering air through which rays of sunlight catch and momentarily illumine vast dogfights of insects and the bright fluttering kites of delicate wings. A garden spellbound. Enchanted as if by more than light, or by divine light. From the darkness of the mound to the great sodden wound in the earth, the red trench and its stony foundations, we are granted passage into an ethereal vista, a world reborn.

As if responsible for this magical conjuring of a natural world more celestial than tropical, a curious monument rears upon the rear lawn of this attractively weathered house. Positioned in the centre of the broad lawn, lying directly south of the mound that huddles beneath the great yew tree, a strange, charred tower looms, skeletal. One constructed recently. Then set alight.

A tall, tilting installation founded on imperial mattresses. An unnatural bed laid for a thicket of chair and table legs that extend like the bony limbs of cattle incinerated in heaps during culls for foot-and-mouth disease. Amidst the vertical sticks of fire-thinned furniture, other items can be identified: the remnants of incinerated picture frames, a bubbled television, a sofa burned to dark scraps hanging from the fine bones of once taut springs. A chaos of other items cindered beyond recognition have also been wedged like stones in a wall, entwined, roped, nailed and jammed, to erect this tower. Lamps, cushions, silken duvets, velvet curtains and electrical appliances serve as additional mortar and kindling.

The conflagration must have been great, snapping at the sky, belching black, caustic smoke as the household's belongings popped, fizzed and split. Overnight, the blaze was dampened by the rain that still bejewels petals and leaves encircling the ruined spire. The pyre is cold and black now. No longer smoking or steaming, it has been transformed into a morbid fossil of once fine household treasures. The purpose of such a focused incineration of furniture, ornaments and appliances is not apparent. But the sooty wreckage serves as a stain upon the beauty of the garden and proclaims a violence, a reminder of the transience of material things, of worldly considerations. There is also a tribal or pagan quality to this arson, as if the construction of the pyre and its subsequent firing symbolised a departure from one place to another, or endowed a transformation from one state to another. A rite seems to have been enacted, a passage begun, a journey taken.

Though to where?

Perhaps a clue will present itself within the circle of bowls placed about the hem of the bonfire. Plain ceramic fruit bowls, transparent mixing bowls, patterned casserole dishes and large steel saucepans have been arranged in a perfect circle about the carbonised spire. These articles stood far enough away from the fire to avoid incineration, though some are sooty on one side. Two empty plastic canisters lie discarded beyond the ring. They are coloured red and appear empty, but the perfume of petroleum lingers on the grass in patches where it was splashed and dribbled.

Circling the bonfire clockwise, the stale scents of cooling plastics, metals and rain-dampened fabrics pierce the sinuses, a sharp toxic cocktail of the chemicals incinerated in the conflagration, though made especially pungent by the underlying fragrance of seared animal flesh.

An aluminium ladder rests against the south side of the pyre. It was used to build the pyre's scaffolding, layer by layer. The side of the ladder facing the conflagration is pitchy, the rubber fittings melted.

Inside the first household container at the foot of the bony spire, the gleam of precious metals is immediately apparent. A woman's jewellery, rings, earrings, necklaces, brooches and watches. Spare change and paper money have also been thrown into a receptacle more often employed for mixing the ingredients for cakes. A metal casserole dish, enamelled red, has proven adequate for storing the household's important papers, the red border of a birth certificate uppermost and topping a sloping stack of share certificates, investment statements, papers related to financial administration, the deeds of the house. A strong wind will blow the records away.

After a large saucepan, in which several glass and ceramic ornaments have been crammed together as if by a refugee fleeing their home before the onslaught of an approaching army, a large suitcase lies closed but unlatched. Hard-shelled, with a set of black wheels in the base, this large item of luggage is most often observed squealing across the concourse of an airport in the wake of a scurrying passenger. But inside this hollow container no clothes or toiletries have been carefully packed and pressed to fit the space. The scent that hangs in a fatty pall about the smeared case has been produced by the fumes of meat cooked and left to cool; the fragrance is the first indicator of the case's unwholesome cargo.

Upon opening the case, it is apparent that what has been crammed inside this receptacle for an altogether more bizarre journey than is usually taken by a traveller is more significant than a collection of carefully selected, valuable belongings. Stored inside the container is the traveller.

The much reduced figure would either have been raked piecemeal from the cinders and clinker of the pyre's blaze, or collected and worked upon so that the cremated, hairless and fleshless remains could all be fitted inside the case. The position suggests the foetal and the infantile, with some appendages detached and placed about the ribby barrel of torso and the still grinning head, sticky and glistening as if recently tarred.

Against the endless fathoms of blue that extend into this day's Olympian canopy, from this position on the lawn beside the extinguished pyre a new distraction becomes apparent: a column of black, oily smoke is burgeoning and unfolding upwards from a neighbouring property, three or four doors down, until the fumes dissipate into a grubby mist that drifts higher in the deliriously sun-burnished air.

If the still serviceable ladder is removed from the bones of the pyre and leant against the hedge on the western border of the garden, there is a view of the neighbouring property. And over the neatly trimmed privet hedge that stands almost three metres tall to maximise privacy, to deflect the wind and noise from elsewhere, a second pyre becomes visible on the neighbour's lawn. Their spire is also of ambitious construction. Two large divan-bed bases form foundations sturdy enough to hold a leather settle and rosewood dining table. Free-standing antique wardrobes crowd two sides, like stokers who must have attended the same flames that eventually consumed them, leaving them doorless.

About this scorched ruin lies another ring of household containers, their contents obscured from this vantage point. Amongst the bowls, plastic planters, a packing crate and a vinyl holdall, a linen trunk is visible. The embroidered fabric is marred by the ugly seepage of its greasy contents.

Beyond the neighbouring pyre, across another perfect pea-green lawn and the equally tonsured hedge, the peak of a third spire is visible. The top of a free-standing lamp thrusts into the air like the burned flagless pole of a decimated army.

Further on from the spindly silhouette of the lamp, a column of smoke spirals to the sky, three gardens down. A smear against a blue ocean of clean air; an industrial brown through which sparks dart like fireflies, seeking oxygen in which to glow brightly and briefly before extinction into falling ash.

Beyond the geyser of grubby smoke, another two parallel plumes drift from the next two gardens.

Within pauses, as the birds inhale before issuing fresh, excitable choruses of whistles and shrieks, the distant clang of a metal ladder becomes faintly audible: a step-ladder being arranged at the foot of another pyre, as yet unlit.

Low Tide

*U*pon the bottom of the swimming pool an obese form squats. Against blue tiles, the bulb's rubbery dimensions suggest the bud of a giant tropical flower, an exotic fruit, or some lambent marine flora glimpsed through the face-mask of a diver drifting along a coral reef.

Closer.

Dotting the smooth bulk, a constellation of lime spots patterns strawberry skin. The sun's power brightens the smooth floor of the pool and flat surface of the water; a taut and motionless membrane above the vast anemone. A creature the size of an armchair, held fast to the slippery tiles by suction. Crowning it, a thicket of fulgent feelers, tinted the pink of candy, are turned inwards to brush and palpate the contents of the corpulent body. Spongy fingers sedately probe and arrange what has been swallowed and now bulges from inside the fleshy bag, a mostly concealed meal. Contracting muscles ripple the pulpy bulk from the root of the stout lump to the filigree of pink strands that work the top. A feeding without mess, an incremental reduction of matter swallowed whole that is both methodical and graceful. Yet a portion of the meal is visible in the ringed mouth of the gleaming bulk. From a pale scalp, a long plume of blonde hair floats like seaweed in a rock pool. Strands separate, catch and reflect the sun's rays. Like golden threads trailing from needles, one by one, the wafting locks are collected by a pink feeler and carefully tucked inside the strawberry sack.

Rising in the water, closer to the surface.

The pool is twenty metres long, ten wide. The water clear but verging on milky at the far edges. Dotted about the ceramic tiles of the rectangular space, six more of the plump masses cling. Each spongy pap gently masticates the contents of its capacious stomach. Two of the creatures appear taller, resemble rosy columns, as if their digestion is more advanced than that of their neighbours. Their pink feelers have resumed a bloom and a seething exploration of the surrounding water, prospecting for more of what has been consumed and now rendered pulpy. From the mouth of the most distant anemone, a pale human forearm extends, the delicate wrist curved gracefully. A diamond ring sparkles upon a slender finger.

Break from the surface and confront a wide, flat area of smooth cement. Arranged around the rectangular pool area, a single row of blue recliners loaf against the perimeter fence. The frames are made from steel, the upholstery plastic. The remainder of the man-made equipment circling this area – the small lifeguard tower, timber picnic tables, tall blue sun umbrellas, steel rails that ascend into the shallow end of the pool, and a scattering of portable white chairs of moulded plastic – is partially obscured by great drapes of seaweed, the texture resembling wool dyed the green of nettles.

A closer inspection of this extensive natural matting will reveal the coarse, dry substance to be similar to *Rhizoclonium* weed. The smell of this green wave is a cocktail of brackish estuary brine and beached, sun-ripened marine life; a stench that oppresses the area wherever the intense nasal spice of chlorine abates. This entire pool area, so carefully decorated blue and white, is gradually being overwhelmed by this hairy blanket of weed. In patches, the necks of plastic bottles protrude from the bristling green tide, as do disparate shoes, a colourful litter of paper, part of a fishing net and two yellow litter bins.

Leaving the pool area through an open gate, furred green, several communal paths remain partially visible betwixt the devouring swamp of stinking seaweed. Outside the pool area, a veritable city of once-white caravans reaches into the distance in three directions.

Looking west and south, row upon row of these discoloured, flat-roofed chalets extends up the sides of hills, about which a flock of sea birds circles and occasionally drops. To the east, suburbs of identical chalets file down the slope towards the misty vista of a grey sea. A solitary two-storey building breaks the monotony: a restaurant, theatre, bar and administration block. Its roof terrace displays a praetorian guard of sun umbrellas, standing to attention above the long tinted windows of the structure's walls. To the north, a high metal fence and a palisade of thick hedges and trees separates the holiday camp from a main road.

With the exception of the flock of birds that hovers above, all remains still at the holiday camp. Nothing visibly moves. But from various directions, muffled sounds carry through the sun-warmed air. Rustles of long forms, moving unseen through dry seaweed, emerge here and there, though the direction of travel, the purpose of the manoeuvres and what is in transit are obscured by the consecutive, unremitting ranks of chalets.

Following the arterial that descends to the administrative and entertainment block, and keeping to the middle of the tarmac roadway, other odd disturbances can be detected within the ranks of chalets flanking this route. From inside a long mobile home, its door ajar, drifts a wet mulching. In another caravan with a gaping door, bumps the flop and thump of a heavy form, as if a tired judo throw is taking place in slow motion. Pause for a few moments and the dragging noise that follows the fleshy thuds implies that a heavy form is being manoeuvred into position upon a hard floor. A noisome sucking sound eventually seeps from this chalet's open door.

The cladding or siding of every chalet within sight of the through-road also bear the marks and stains of what could be mistaken for neglect. Row after row, cul-de-sac after cul-de-sac, from the more expensive cedar homes atop the hills, with decks providing the best sea-views, to the standard forty-foot caravans, not a single dwelling has escaped the markings of a curious and unsightly contamination. The cleaner, brighter vestiges of the walls and the clarity of the pool's water, however, suggest that this transformation has not been the result of a lengthy abandonment or dereliction. Rather, a recent reclamation is indicated by the contrasts of the clean sidings to those places given over to the weed. The land and its structures seem not to fully recognise, nor acknowledge, the suddenness of their transfiguration. They seem to be half what they had until recently been, and half something else entirely. Here exists a condition of modification.

Rashes of what resemble acorn barnacles have spread up the sides of these chalets, consuming the lower third of each. Crustaceans that are pale-blue and grey in colour, some circled by faint pink bands. Assisting the weed's conversion of the planes and right angles to lumpy, bedraggled distortions, these barnacles now form a new cladding upon the holiday cabins, uneven but spreading in continents of shell. In the small apertures, or eyes, that can be observed within the lumpy surface of the crustaceans' coats, glisten small, black fleshy shapes, the size of raisins. The flesh has the texture of snails or molluscs. Looking along the side of an individual chalet unit, the new surface of the outer walls also appears, from some angles, to be whiskered by small transparent cilia that extend from the inhabitants of the shells and appear to stroke the air. Some of the feelers have snared flies.

Some of the caravans possess a parking space at one side; elsewhere, there are small car parks at the ends of the rows of chalets. The scattering of vehicles has been similarly consumed by layers of crustacean. Wherever there was painted metal or glass, silvery barnacles now spread to coat the surfaces in the same manner as they encrust the steel hulls of idle ships. Not all of the shells have hardened. Some remain gelid and moist. Those still forming advance onto any uncovered surface on the vehicles, on railings, television aerials, satellite dishes, washing lines, bicycles. White spongy forms can also be observed in disparate patches about the abandoned vehicles.

Closer examination will reveal mystifying collaborations in the eruption of this ecosystem. The whitish creatures, resembling common sea slugs, crawl around the calcifying shells of the foetal barnacles, their rhinophores busily working the air. Along their wet flanks, a phalanx of soft white feelers sweep like the oars of Athenian galleys, nudging the pale invertebrates along the doors and windscreens of the cars.

If the sun-baked stench can be withstood, inside the nearest accessible chalet, an unusual addition to the plain papered interiors waits to be discovered: an extraordinary decoration of spiny starfish upon the walls and ceiling. Arranged in haphazard constellations, scores of these tiny five-fingered echinoderms have adhered, spider-like, to the walls, cabinet doors and fixed furniture.

The carpet tiles of the floors are sodden with dirty water, suggesting that a flood or spring tide recently receded. The bedrooms, kitchen-dining area and living room are littered by whatever clothes, toiletries, kitchenware and so forth became trapped after the waters lowered. Considering the masses of weed outside and the multitude of spiky starfish in just one dwelling, it's not hard to conjure a clearer picture of a great soupy wave, teeming with strange life, that washed through this holiday camp, and perhaps suddenly, and left so much behind when the waters drained: a vast diversity of life that clamped, adhered and clawed its way onto any available mooring.

The rapidity of the water's advance is attested to by the contents of the master bedroom in this caravan. The elderly owners remain there, though each body lies upon the floor and has suffered mutilation. Their bloodless faces still wear the sleeping masks they wore to bed on what they assumed was another ordinary night. The bedclothes have been torn away by the flow that must have passed through this space. Any items remaining in the wardrobe and drawers now drip and assault the senses with the pungency of an estuary at low tide. The force and suddenness of the tidal surge surely surprised these people when it was too late to make any kind of escape.

More careful examination of the human remains on the wet and refuse-strewn floor of the room reveals evidence that the couple were restrained against their will. Their flesh is blanched and radiates an unhealthy pallor, tinged blue about the mouths and eyelids. Each mouth gapes and is missing false teeth. But the remaining flesh upon the upper chest, shoulders, arms, throat and genital area is perforated by numerous rings of circular black incisions. Only the abdomens are entirely broken open, and inside these even a cursory inspection will reveal the clusters of translucent depositions. Egg cases, almost identical in shape to those of the common cat shark and yet the size of an average human foot. The fibrous strings at either end of the cases have entwined about the lower ribs of the hosts, so that the see-through parcel can hatch within the softer area of the gut; probably the best food source for such impressive parasites.

Inside each egg case, the unhatched occupant appears to be a coiled worm of a startling aquamarine hue. Not dissimilar to the common paddleworm, these segmented bodies would, when unravelled, already stretch to a metre or more in length. And although the tangled passengers appear idle, every few minutes a contraction or convulsion occurs within the transparent egg cases. The visible heads of the unborn worms bear dorsal cilia and frontal horns about circular mouths, indicating that the entire length of the worms supports an intestinal tract. Bristly hairs and unformed scales line the dorsal areas; the ventral area, where visible, is caterpillared with filaments.

Outside the chalet, walking east, the colour of the weed draping each caravan changes in colour, texture and form. Blood-red *Rhodophyta* has extended wherever there were large communal bins, skips and toilet blocks, from which it cascades like swamp grass in a bayou. Almost entirely coating what was once a row of gleaming luxury chalets, each separated from its neighbour by a small ranch fence, a variety of *Cladophora* has wound like feather boas, from which items of clothing and even an ironing board have come to be supported.

Further east, where almost nothing remains uncovered by the weed and quickly forming barnacle beds, the poles supporting the camp's lights and public address system now veritably pulsate and shimmer with the soft white bodies of sea squirts the size of grapefruit. Those at the top of the fleshy columns resemble the Neptune's Heart squirt, though these topmost creatures have achieved the size of huge cauliflowers and have even managed to seize passing or roosting gulls. Red legs and cruel yellow beaks, parted to utter final cries, regularly protrude from the flask-shaped squirts as if the creatures have engaged in an ironic role reversal and swallowed more than they can chew.

But the most remarkable display of carnivorous rapacity performed by the marine life invading the holiday camp is concentrated in the amusement arcade, an enclosed area offering protection from the fierce midday sunlight and built within the ground floor of the large administrative and entertainment block.

Inside the arcade, the electric lights are out. Two rows of upright cabinets of inoperable slot machines and twopenny games are visible, as well as three glass cases piled high with soft toys tempting the metal claws of tiny cranes. Extending into the darkness of the floor, numerous naked and twisted human forms lie inert.

Withered skin sagging and wrinkling about the skeletal structure, a young male left at the foot of a tabletop arcade game looks partially deflated, his flesh bearing the circular patterns of punctures. A glance is sufficient to suggest the body's fluids have been efficiently drained through the puncture rings.

Merely standing close to the makeshift mortuary or lair in which the most available food source has been collected and stored, summons movement from deeper within the unlit building.

Against the tinted window a sudden thump.

Impressed, slug-like, on the other side of the dark glass, the underside of a vivid orange form adheres and lengthens. A worm. At its plumpest, the trunk possesses the thickness of a soil pipe. Segmentation tiles the visible body, soon tapering to a tail obscured in darkness. The creature's size is impressive, because only the mid-section sucks the glass; the head that flops wetly into the doorway must be supported by a further three metres of tubular trunk.

Along the paler underside of the vast worm, a myriad shrimp-coloured spikes protrude from oval sockets. Against the glass the barbels rake and scratch deep, etching a track. Where they touch the floor, the talons pierce the carpet tiling and propel the worm forward, stretching it to an even greater length. What is also surprising is the speed with which the head then turns towards the light, revealing a moist nest of white tentacles the colour of a lobster's flesh, to which a sweet wrapper and a paper cup have adhered like insects to flypaper. As the creature widens and exposes a barbed gullet the colour of an earthworm, the slits of gills on either side of the head also open and slap, open and slap, in a haste of excitement.

Moving away from the arcade and heading further east until knee-deep in serrated and bladderwrack weed, the shoreline becomes visible. Between two caravans in the final row of stained chalets that once enjoyed sea-views, powdery dunes the colour of unbleached sugar hump like the heads of giants trying to hide; forms whose positions are given away by the coarse grasses spiking from their rotund heads.

A wide sandy expanse, glimmering and moist, appears between the hummocks of dune. A distant tide-line froths silver-white. Beyond the foam, the foggy grey air and a dismal sea suggest that matter, and even the known world, are disintegrating into gaseous oblivion.

Breaking from the regimental rows of the caravan park and the stifling unlit confines of the ruins, the reek of decomposing shellfish along the shoreline verges on becoming unbearable. And before progressing further than a few steps beyond the dunes, a great devastation becomes apparent, littering the length and breadth of the exposed beach: a vast array of refuse, flotsam and driftwood stained by sand and mud. Much of the litter is now re-clothed in ill-fitting robes of seaweed.

A fishing vessel lies on its side, bow thrust upward as if the ship is concussed but determined to right itself. Crewless decks are spattered with estuary mud, the remaining windows forming sightless black eyes. Rust-patterned, much of the hull is exposed, the deck and masts forlorn and draped in weed. Near the stern, the lopsided box of a caravan tilts. A collapsing house of buckled playing cards, the front hanging free as if from a solitary hinge.

Dragged here or washed up from further along the coast, a plethora of shards from small boats, planks, fencing, fishing nets, a child's swing set of yellow tubular steel, a bloated sofa, a length of timber banisters, the door of a beach hut, are strewn before the dunes as if belched out by a hurricane. North and south, the same messy collage of ruin and destruction stretches as far as sight will allow until the grey slither of an estuary channel to the north ends the devastation, while a crumbling peninsula of eroding cliffs encases it to the south.

So much to stare at, aghast, particularly at the shoreline half a kilometre away where overlapping waves gush across dark sand as the tide turns. There, a half-collapsed house appears to have found new, temporary foundations upon the shifting sands: the remains of a bungalow, unmoored and swept here. Grey and tiled, the roof appears impossibly straight despite bulging walls. Above this sodden ruin, several pale forms hover. They fight the breeze to maintain position. Airborne objects easily mistaken, at a glance, for kites flown by children, the strings tied to the broken house. Or the swaying lumps might resemble plastic bags, or misshapen seabirds with their wings spread wide. But the drifters all trail white tendrils into the jagged flotsam of the displaced building.

Closer, and identification of the strange airborne lumps becomes easier while disbelief increases. The swaying forms, trailing their near imperceptible ribbons inside the bungalow, gain sufficient definition to indicate an artificial or rubbery texture. The largest form within this drifting flock resembles a bell-shaped bag, with transparent skirts and a heart, or brain, the colour of a tangerine.

Closer still, and it becomes clear that these are hydrozoans, or jellyfish: nine in number, each swaying in the manner of a drift upon the surface of a gusty sea, though here the creatures roll with air currents, not surges of seawater. Employing a variety of long and short tentacles, dangling like rags of jelly, the gelid flock fastidiously explores broken sections of wood, buckled metal and windowless frames. At its new address, the wreck of a home is being picked over.

One lozenge-shaped float, its translucent flesh a pinkish hue, trails curly tendrils through the holed eaves. Another fleshy bag, an opaque form the size of a fully-grown cow, displaying a bruised crest similar to the Portuguese Man-of-war, has taken advantage of a missing door to insert its ventral draperies inside the dark spaces of this home that was dragged here by the flood.

The largest of these creatures possesses the wide blue skirts of the By-the-wind sailor jellyfish, the body stretching two metres from one end of the disc to the other. A glistening marvel that has raised its puffy vertical sail to add stability to its drift amid the sea's breezes. Two of its appendages stir, or maybe feel about, in the crushed domestic rooms below.

And closer still, where the frantic scuffling of what might be a dog's paws and a piteous whine become audible, it is possible to deduce that any living thing that might have crawled inside any section of the broken house would have inevitably come into contact with the investigative sweeping of the fleshy ribbons that droop from the undulating petticoats above. Driven to seek refuge below deck, neither man nor beast could avoid the probing, poisonous tentacles for long. Even now it is not difficult to imagine the exploratory prodding and predatory probing of the strips of jellied flesh, inside collapsed rooms, eager to locate the frightened animals below, their cries raising not a twitch of remorse from these semi-transparent hunters of the shoreline.

And yet, so close to the abrasive scrape of the small waves at the tideline, the greatest revelation of this much-changed coastal area awaits discovery. Only the cursory inspection of a visitor unfamiliar with this coastline would mistake that large form, one kilometre out at sea, for an island. To eyes shaded from the intensity of the sun that now arcs to the west and sits overhead, eyes gazing directly at the distant surface of the vast protuberance, this monument, this recent addition to the horizon, is resplendent. Arrayed like spines across its crest and the rounded sides, a forest of spikes radiate a purple hue whenever the cloud cover parts. And thousands of these bristling appendages extend from the spherical rocky surface of the vast object. Though the dimensions of the island make a comparison absurd, the form does resemble the common Purple Heart Urchin, a small sea creature often abandoned by the sea at low tide, or marooned after fierce gales that batter shorelines.

Dead centre of the sphere, a black hole, like a red-rimmed mouth, small at this distance, is visible in the spiny wall. An aperture pursed as if to whistle. This perforation, this vent, is dark inside. An orifice offering access to the vast interior, or escape from inside the gargantuan housing of the shell.

To the south and down the coast, though much reduced in size by distance, another vast sea-urchin shape squats immobile at the far end of the beach. Beyond the rocky peninsula and further out to sea, a third is visible, its dimensions more oval at such a remove.

Each of these gigantic structures remains immobile. Implacable as lonely atolls and arranged in a curious armoured archipelago, they appear anchored to the seabed and braced rigid to withstand turbulence and tide. And the longer they are observed, the more the huge spheres resemble the landing craft of a seaborne invasion fleet from a war long past. Vessels idling upon grim seas after discharging their complements, their successive waves of conquering warriors. Perhaps these sea-urchin spheres are more numerous too. It is not impossible to imagine these spiny sentinels occupying a frontline that reaches for hundreds of kilometres, all situated strategically wherever the fishing inland is good.

Hold the World in My Arms for Three Days and All Will Be Changed.

In the Night

*O*bservable from the window of this cottage is a moon stained the red of a white pebble inside a glass of red wine. About this celestial body and across the entirety of a sky blushed crimson, iron booms. A great pealing of bells. A multitude of distant church bells, all ringing and clamouring. An ominous, discordant clanging that falls from where the intense scarlet light issues. But raising unshaded eyes to glimpse whatever is responsible for irradiating and deafening the night is too painful.

Below the window of this cottage, shadows harden treacle-black. Tarmac, paving stones, houses, gardens, border walls, hedgerows and vehicles are dyed merlot. Autumnal russets shimmer the trees and hedgerows.

Elsewhere in the blooded canopy, on the other side of the red night sky, where the sun would rise to burn by day in the east, there hangs a sense, more than the sight, of new, vast dimensions and the monumental weight of another object oppressing the atmosphere. A shape defined by a blocking-out of the stars. An uneven silhouette so high above. Gigantic, black, inert, occulted by blood-light.

Third Day

This room is cold. Early sun streams bright against closed windows and curtains. Daylight stronger than usual, no longer red but the white of burning phosphorus, now contaminates the sealed darkness. Drives spikes betwixt the curtains and wall.

Outside, the world is mute as if all activity has been suspended in one of those rare pauses that occurs at first light, or after midnight. The soundless dormancy elongates, is unwilling to cease.

The bed and air are rank, the room needs airing, the discarded bedclothes on the floor need burning.

A glass of water on the bedside table. About it sachets of cold and flu remedy lie scattered among blister-packs of painkillers. The outline of a missing body remains impressed into a sordid mattress. Beside the bed, soiled towels lie strewn like rags washed in by a septic tide. They cover a brown plastic washing-up bowl, the splashed contents obscured.

The empty silence of the unheated house stretches away from the bed, this room. Without warmth, the old cottage smells damp, dusty, is spiced with the taint of old paintwork. Another time already appears to have superimposed itself upon the interior: one many years into the future of its coming dereliction, or a time from the house's past when the building lay empty before.

Downstairs, it is easy to imagine the ground floor of the cottage now appearing as unfamiliar to its former owner as it would have done following a long trip away from home. The same place but starker, the unfamiliar taking time to incrementally become familiar in a light brighter and more bleaching and crueller in its revelation of neglect. The front door has been left wide open. Whoever departed left this house unbarred some time ago. Wet verdure, damp cement and wood, the scents of outdoors encroach across the carpets, as does the sickly incandescence.

Inside a small kitchen exists evidence of a life during the onset of illness: a pan encrusted with whitish soup, gritty with desiccated chives. A cupboard door gapes where a drinking glass was clutched to wash down tablets. A grimy ceramic dessert bowl, cemented with bran flakes from the last breakfast, crisps inside the dry sink. Milk curdles vanilla where slopped. A cabinet is bearded with soup the colour of magnolia emulsion. The blind or concussed appear to have scrabbled here, too preoccupied with their suffering to clean.

The clock on the wall softly clicks, an unobtrusive metronome, still on duty despite the abandonment. 08:25am is the time.

No post.

The continuing silence, the strange sense of an absence of energy and motion outside the building, frames and emphasises the emptiness and stillness within. In such thick, cold air pierced with arctic light, time moves like the swell of a sea. Only delicate, simple movements seem possible or appropriate, as if a body must adjust to an unfamiliar gravity.

Looking from the kitchen window, over the lawn, the pavement, the road, the hedges and bushes of the front gardens across the road, three of the four visible front doors are open.

A cold morning, and yet no one appears to close these gaping doors. Nor is anyone busy in their garden, or washing a car, leaving for work, guiding a child to school or walking a dog. No one is visible in the street at all. No vehicles swish past.

Minutes drift by and the odd stasis mocks, communicating that nothing will change, no matter how long this street is watched.

Observable from the kitchen window, deeper inside the close where the road turns, another two receptions expose themselves. Inside each visible open door, electric light shines dimly but is overcome by the dazzling albescence that illumines the distant shapes of coats on racks, side-tables, discarded shoes, square mats for wiping feet.

All of the driveways before all of the visible buildings reveal cars frosted in a cold blaze of the curious daylight, all parked as they would be during the evening. More vehicles than usual slump kerbside. No one left home this morning.

Towards the end of the cul-de-sac, at the T-junction, another three white facades of larger, newer houses appear eerily unwelcoming despite their unobstructed entrances.

Outside the cottage, on the front lawn, a breeze rattles the leaves on the solitary palm that yearns south. A bird shrieks in the distance. The only sounds. And again there is a lonesome, pained cry from the gull, as mournful as a lone survivor disinterring itself from rubble. Though nothing here is broken or appears damaged.

On the pavement before the cottage, there should be the sound of near continuous traffic. No more than fifty metres from this village street, a ring road slices the chilled fields and frigid valleys and would normally produce the song of a distant body of water, an ocean or fast-flowing river, all day and for most of each evening, only ceasing at night when the journeys cease. There is no traffic now. The faraway swish of tyres on tarmac is completely absent at 8:30am: one of the busiest times of day, the school run. Where are the zoo noises of capering children?

The airy spaces outside the cottage seem larger, more open. Stand here long enough and a longing for the bark of a dog, the grunt of a lawnmower or the urgent hum of a car engine is understandable. But only palm fronds softly clatter and a far-off hungry bird caws once more before drifting out of earshot.

It appears that much was taken away from here. Is missing. Removed. Though much remains and is recognisable.

Cross the silent road and approach the house opposite. Stand in the porch. Peek inside the gullet of papered walls, the contents of picture frames indistinct, an ornamental barometer beside a rack of keys. Ring the bell and wait awkwardly in uncomfortable expectation as if watched from within. Wait and wait until no one comes.

Step inside.

Living room and kitchen and dining room compel a glance. Walls cluttered with prints, line drawings, family photographs. Newspapers abound upon chairs and a table: fragile records of recent times unrecoverable. A kitchen clean and empty save for curling crusts and two scraped tins on a breadboard.

Up the stairs.

She's been in this room for some time, all alone.

The curtains are closed. Heavy wooden furniture, a wardrobe and cluttered dressing table, contribute to the oppressive gloom. Stale air, betraying a hint of perfumed hand-cream, an elderly woman's exhalations and the peculiar stifling scent of this home, is now succumbing to the scent of a damp lawn. The front door has been open long enough for the cold air to invade the hallway, stairs and empty rooms, to defeat the central heating's homely warmth. The chilled air of a new dawn is winning here.

The lady sits upright. A large headrest of pillows sandbags her back and shoulders. Her wheelchair waits beside the bed, an obedient, patient companion ready to offer service. Packets of medication litter the bedside table. Jug of water, empty.

The woman's inert and scruffy white head is turned to the curtains. Her hair hasn't seen a comb in a while, is ghost white and thinning about a pink scalp. A baby bird abandoned in a nest. Most of the blue in those startled irises has leaked from the lifeless, rheumy eyes. Bloodshot whites have also soured yellow as if a liver within her scrawny body shrivelled and failed. Fragile stick-limbs and collar bones that might have been whittled behind the wire of a penal camp indent the white nightgown. A face as wrinkled as wet linen sags grey.

A shard of icy light stabs through a parting in the curtains. Dust reels.

The cluttered room hasn't been redecorated in a long time. White and gold wallpaper is mismatched with the worn red carpet. Disparately coloured towels, bedclothes and messy clumps of clothing form mounds and molehills across floor-space not already buried by the enormous bed and bulky furniture.

A lifeless woman in her bed. Outside, the quiet village streets. Each front door open or half open. No one, no traffic.

Wander

At the first junction on the ring road two roads cross. Traffic lights change meaninglessly. No one waits on red.

Across the road an untidy smattering of businesses in cement buildings are corralled within moats of unadorned grass and empty carparks, fenced by streetlights. Cuboid superstores wait to open, the storefronts dark, doors closed.

Gutters and verges of the dual carriageway are littered with plastic until the next town begins and the first abandoned car becomes visible, blocking the left-hand lane with the driver's side door open, headlights on.

An unremarkable interior gives no indication why the vehicle was abandoned.

Directly ahead of the vehicle another set of traffic lights changes colours dutifully for motorists who never arrived this morning.

Towards the town.

White, near identical houses, more traffic islands. Nothing moves. A featureless cement college, another utilitarian retail park and one hotel, windows mostly unlit, their car parks empty. A child's toy town of white and grey bricks, abandoned when interest waned.

This road should be busy at this time. Traffic only thins here around 10pm, when the supermarkets close. Up to midnight, some motorists would also drive home from late shifts or evenings out. Whatever occurred to empty the village and the town's surrounding roads must have occurred in the early hours, when the sole motorist was using this particular stretch of road.

No amount of gaping into the stillness, nor urging the silence to break, will force this world to speak.

The natural light at this time of day and the clarity of the air remain noticeably odder. Where the road widens to four lanes and the land flattens for the retail developments, few trees have survived. Being more exposed, the anomalies of the atmospherics are more apparent in such a wide space. Though low grey cloud covers the entire sky from horizon to horizon, and though no breath of wind stirs the monotony, the pearly luminance of the hidden sun and all it reveals is far brighter than it should be. Masonry and road markings glare as white as new marble.

Sound should carry from afar too, but there is nothing, not even the gull.

Two more abandoned cars on the main road that sluices into the town, driver's side doors open, headlights on.

A window, or windscreen, smashes. Somewhere in the distance the sinister sound of breaking glass shatters the silence. A noise to ice a scalp, splintering from inside the town.

Does glass break of itself in abandoned places? Can material objects fall apart so quickly after dereliction? People break things like windows and bottles. People. Usually younger people, boys or teens. Bored and angry males, men. Are people here?

So from which direction did the noise splinter? Turn and follow the memory of the direction from which glass exploded.

Head into an estate of terraced or semi-detached houses. A working-class area. Concrete homes built on hills for workers in the '70s to support industries long closed. Everywhere, homes crammed together, curbs choked with vehicles parked bumper-to-bumper on narrow roads. And every visible door on the main road, and within the interconnecting side streets and the culs-de-sac, gapes open. Here it is empty too. Emptied. A world entirely silent save one broken window that has left the still air taut with suspense, or in anticipation of something. Anything.

Nothing. The memory of a pane of glass breaking grows disconnected from the deserted, pale aisles of family homes and abandoned cars. A cemetery missing its beloved. Until . . .

There. Up there. Not for long. A black shape falling upwards and showing against the white glare that burns through the smothering blanket of low bright cloud cover. What is it? Resembles . . . a body? Dropping into the atmosphere at a sickening speed until the flopping limbs shrink into a black shape and a flap of cloth like a small flag in high wind. The form quickly becomes a mere grain, and finally nothing, in the bright magnesium air.

A falling body? One pulled, perhaps, or sucked upwards as if gravity momentarily failed in a particular place in the silent town. From over there, somewhere near the smashed window, the body fell up.

Down a long residential canyon, the long silence resuming, towards the place the silent loose-limbed figure appeared to shoot upwards into the sky. Up a side street lined with three-bedroom houses, the white rendering removed to reveal red bricks on two properties.

There, over there: a house with empty window-frames on the first floor, facing the street. Long shards of double-glazed glass shimmer on the neat grass of a front lawn and across an uneven cement drive upon which a blue VW is parked. Two large panes of glass have been pushed through from inside the house. One PVC frame has dropped and demolished the roses under the front windows.

Up a path of tilting stone slabs to the open front door. Heaps of coats suffocate a coatrack, a plastic telephone clings to the wall at the foot of the stairs.

Living room. The room is tidy.

A sewing box and cloth bag filled with knitting are neatly arranged on a small table beside a recliner chair. Puzzle magazines and a stack of library romances build a symmetrical pillar on the coffee table. A cluster of remote control handsets slot into a special holder. An elderly woman or couple lived here.

Photographs of children and middle-aged people with dated haircuts festoon one wall and the mantel. Family pictures taken years before. The faces of the children from the past can be matched to the modern portraits of three teenagers. A large print of a harbour on one wall above a gas fire with an ornate front.

The kitchen itself appears new; the kitchenware is white, the crockery patterned with pink flowers in bows.

More pictures, ornaments, fishing trophies and lots of crystal inside cabinets fixed to the walls of a cramped dining room. A tidy garden out back, the daffodils already blooming. Ordinary, orderly, tidy senior citizens lived here.

The back door in the dining room leads to a locked conservatory. Keys hang from the lock. Same for the outer conservatory door. If a person was responsible for breaking the upstairs windows they either will still be inside the house or recently left the property through the open front.

Upstairs. A wheelchair lift, the chair poised for descent at the summit of the short staircase.

A little box room on the left. Inside, a small table, a sewing machine, a wardrobe.

Then a spare bedroom across the landing. Inside, a single bed, fitted wardrobes, a dressing table, mirror. Empty of life.

Silver light streams through the broken windows and blanches the third bedroom, the master bedroom, to reveal a duvet drooping like a big white tongue from the mattress to the floor. There is a pillow on the floor and a plastic cup. The carpet is wet, maybe with water from the beaker. A bedside table is littered with medication packets and a medicine bottle. A walking frame lies upon its side. An elderly invalid was ill here. The curtains are torn down and cower in clumps.

Inside the fitted wardrobes: clothes inside polythene, racks of shoes, jigsaw puzzles, not enough room for someone to hide.

Turn and leave. Nothing here, no answers.

Into the street. The front of each property, the murky windows, the open doors, neat lawns and closed back gates, but no signs of occupation.

Let the search continue within a situation never failing to be preposterous. More houses. In and out. Go inside these private, hitherto hidden domains of strangers. Tasteful interiors, or aged and neglected living spaces, the furniture they used, their massive televisions, the hoarding of photographs of those they loved, the odd kitchen better suited to a celebrity's home, their extensions, gardens, children's toys, the weird domestic fragrances enduring through dereliction. Once mysterious inner worlds hidden behind plain facades seen thousands of times, but unknowable until now, until this.

Empty spaces. All of the beds unmade. No signs of people packing in a hurry as would be expected in the homes of the evacuated. The doors of cupboards and wardrobes are closed as are the drawers of cabinets. No half-filled suitcases. Cars haven't moved from their night-time moorings.

Only in one kitchen does a gas ring burn. Someone had been warming milk in a pan on a stove before being interrupted, before leaving. The stench of the blackened pan was noticeable from the pavement outside.

An event occurring in the early hours of the morning might also account for the lack of oven activity as well as the plethora of parked private vehicles. Perhaps the milk was being heated in the pan by a night owl too preoccupied to turn off the stove before they walked out of their life, along with their neighbours. No one turned off their central heating. Internal thermostats automatically reacted to doors left open and fired up boilers. Few lights remain switched on. They'd either been switched off as people left their homes or had never been switched on at all during the evacuation. So did the thousands of people who lived in this town and the nearby village stealthily shuffle out of their homes, in their nightclothes, at the same time, in the dark?

To go where?

The dead woman in her bed in the village, an invalid. The town house with broken windows contained a wheelchair and stair-lift. When most of the population left home, maybe some of the infirm were stranded? Still, no real answers present themselves. No knowing. No understanding. Just *this*.

Walk, walk, walk. More of *this*.

Two schools, internally gloomy behind rings of forbidding steel fencing. Play parks empty, the metal climbing equipment barren, stark and forlorn before dusty hedges. A shuttered health centre and small local supermarket where the town ends. At the boundary, a featureless patchwork of arable fields consumes the land. No cows, no sheep. Empty pastures rise over distant hills.

The air perceptibly chills without any additional assistance from a wind. Stills but swiftly grows cold and begins to attempt the creation of a winter scene on a greeting card.

From above drift a myriad flakes, sauntering from the ceiling of low, bright cloud, which has been pierced since dawn by the white, chemical intensity of light. Now, in places where the cloud cover is thinnest, tinges of gold and pink bleed through. Here and there, a dirty reddish tint. A trace of mauve. Until now, the day has been cool but mild, the air unmoving. Now it is freezing and snowing.

Afternoon: Back to the Village

Snow. Pristine. Snow has fallen before the open doors to form drifts blocking front steps. Still, no vehicles move; no voices sound. No visible indentations of footsteps on the pavement or the drives of the houses. The street, gardens, roofs, cars and lawns are blanketed with thick snow, a white surface unbroken. The world is white, yet the very air possesses a rosy patina. Between the eaves, under the vehicles and at the foot of the hedges, the world is inked black.

Directly above, what was a reddish smudge on the sky at the edge of the town has spread here as if a distant sun is bleeding heavily and steadily into clouds heavy with snow.

Things are changing here.

Broken glass outside the cottage where the dead woman was found sitting up and waiting in her bed. The front windows of the first floor of her house are now empty black sockets. Several panes of glass have been reduced to icy shards and lie scattered across the front lawn and drive.

Inside the cottage, the woman's bed is now empty. Pillows are scattered and her bedclothes hang like sails without wind from the empty window frames of her bedroom. The lifeless woman from this room has been discharged.

Through the windowless frames and looking north, an alarming mist of black, oily smoke drifts into view. The smoke much thicker where the road turns.

Out of the cottage and up the road towards the smoke. A dull roar and a snapping and crackling of tinder grow louder.

Here is the fire with flames beating orange beneath a plume of impenetrable black smoke: a house at the end of the lane with its roof ablaze. Near the conflagration the freezing air reeks of melted plastic and chemicals.

A privet hedge crowns the front garden of the burning house. A newer house than most here, with four bedrooms. Only the roof burns but all of the windows upstairs and downstairs are knocked out: double-glazed windows, not smashed but pushed out entirely and lying intact on the lawn within PVC frames. Maybe there had been a build-up of gas in the empty building; perhaps an explosion forced the windows out.

From the pavement, at the end of the front path leading to a front door cast wide, a flurry of movement deeper inside the house distracts. Movement near the ceiling of the front room.

Through the gaping hole where the bay windows should be, a dim interior is partially visible: the black rectangle of a picture on a wall, the sketchy fronds of house plants resembling blackened crops, a bulky sofa, the glimpse of a white garden out back.

Light falling into the burning and smoke-filled spaces of the building is reflected by the motion of a pale form, suspended beneath a magnolia ceiling. The figure hangs or appears to hover. About the form, something droops like a bird's broken wing. A white dressing gown.

Sparks and black debris from the roof drop, sizzling as they cool in the snow on the front lawn. Closer to the empty window frames, the interior is better revealed: muted beige colours, a wooden table, sideboard. And the figure of a man hanging from the ceiling.

He is horizontal.

An elderly man near the rafters. Thin-faced, the mouth ajar, unblinking eyes aghast in a lifeless face twisted by terror and bafflement at the moment of death. Perhaps this man was rendered helpless and held aloft, as if he were being toyed with, until his death. Thin arms and legs flop from their sockets suggesting that he is lying across a chair in midair. Yet nothing supports his body from below; the dining room and rear garden are clearly visible beneath the suspended corpse. Chest and head mere inches from the ceiling, the man's entire form sways as if upon the gentle swell of water.

So is he fixed to the ceiling? The body's position and situation are absurd and horribly ridiculous, as if an elaborate and grotesque prank is being played within.

A few seconds more, then the body drops, or is dropped. A sudden, terrible plummet resulting in a *whump* and woody crack below the windowless rectangle in the exterior wall.

Fire cracks a joist above, roof tiles spit. Black debris drops from the guttering in sooty skirts. Like volcanic ash, smoke unfurls across the perfectly white-sheeted lawn. Behind the opaque veil of soot and shadow, new movement. Frantic motion, as if a cat, more of shadow than sinew and limb, were thrashing a mouse about the floor.

The bumping and cracking of lifeless limbs in a confined space follows, until the old body seems to enact an escape: to loll, then thrash its arms over the sill of the empty window casements. Then the body is gone, so fast, a stone dropped into an ocean of blood high above the house, the village, the world.

Look up, try to follow the flailing figure growing tiny in seconds. Head and limbs in a brief flap of a robe that resembles a failed parachute, but soon detaches from the body and seems to hang in the air to watch its recent occupant disappear further into clouds as crimson as the interior of some vast, skinless body.

A man, a toy, a miniature, a black dot, flung away so deeply into the scarlet atmosphere. Gone. All gone.

Look down. Inside the house, only smoke and flames move.

More smoke. Near and far. Brown and dirty and flowing high into the air across the village. Sundered timbers and bursting plasterboards start to crack gunshots through the cold, scarlet air.

In the village, more and more of the white buildings huddle beneath columns of the black smoke sluicing from their dirty, fire-plumed hats. Long pillars of smoke growing more numerous and intensifying as the empty village is put to the torch. Above, the dense cloud cover has grown redder; natural light now filters through a lens the colour of rose-water. Where the cloud breaks into platelets and continents drifting apart like melting ice, the frayed edges are tinged pink. In between the disintegrating clouds, the skies' wounds are tinted like blood lacking oxygen.

The sky reddens from horizon to horizon. Charcoal fumes spiral, unhindered by air currents. Until, over there, another body. Up, up, up it goes, so fast as if flung from hidden artillery on the ground. Unresisting and cartwheeling upwards, the velocity growing, the urgency of the silhouette's vertical plummet is breathtaking.

And another, northwest, just visible but no bigger than a black pebble whizzing from a slingshot into the red sky. Those left behind reclaimed. Where they resided set alight.

Evening: Red Sky at Night, Shepherd's Delight

Nature peels away the old skin of winter's baffling resurgence. A freak summer commences.

Twilight is distinguished by rubescent light and a sudden swelling warmth. Humid air swiftly pockmarks and perforates the snow cover that has been unbroken since midday. Florid pavements and burgundy tarmac road surfaces appear; the gutters are blackened by melt-water. The chill steams and disperses in such tropical temperatures.

Beyond the village, the land inexplicably melts like a cake left uncovered and without shade. The green space and tarmac winding away from the village are soon patchworked by the sudden heat into drying bands of blood-lit snow, glistening tributaries, beautiful hell trees, pastures of gore, dewy glimmers infernal. Kermes, carmine, alizarin: the surface of another planet. Snow on a May morning, midsummer by dusk.

Turn to the north, to the white blocks of the town. The smoking chimneys of local industries long extinct might have reopened to demonstrate peak production. A murky cumulus of toxic smoke flows upwards and billows across the surrounding hills. Pollutants from the burning town disperse into the growing, unnerving, ruddy stains of the sky, wiping soot on florid cheeks. Above the town and village the skies' wounds worsen, the scarlet taint horrible, the low cloud as blackened as unchanged cotton wool pressed to burns. From the inferno, tiny indefinable forms occasionally fall at the sky. Tiny cinders, eager to catch up with those who left earlier.

But move away from the reek of burning chemicals, melted plastic and seared timber, to this building that is not yet a pyre. Move to the first building beyond the burning village and the smoke-belching town: a period building, a former country estate, once a private school, now a luxury residential care home. A final beacon without flames, a last redoubt at the end of the earth.

A scattering of cedars and pines extend around the grounds of the care home. A regal drive passes along a tree-smothered lane, wide enough for one vehicle. The front gates of the entrance are open.

Into the wooded estate through shards of light tinged pink, slicing the foliage and blushing the floor of the surrounding woodland. Rapidly melting snow shows tints of indigo, a violet shimmer. Lumps of melt dot the drive like a heavy, littering blossom. The approach to an enchanted wedding in a fairytale and to the great white building that soon appears between parting trees. A place where the elderly came to die in comfort, their deadlines brought forward now.

Blood in snow. The land's new sinister beauty encourages suspicions of an atmosphere that has been replaced by another; one too strange for the consequences of an event or catastrophe caused by mankind. The light, the surfaces of things, seem transported from another place in the cosmos. Within this vivid new spectrum of colour, what other changes have occurred that cannot be seen?

Out of the aisle of overhanging trees, their myriad leaves jewelled by garnets of melting snow, diamante sparkles drip-drip from encroaching branches. Ivy-covered stables rear on one side, buildings repurposed for the residents' communal activities. The lights are on.

From within the main building music plays, something classical. Has it played relentlessly, day and night, since *the event*? The wide front doors within the grandiose columns of the Doric *porte-cochère* were swung wide some time before and have not been closed. Darkness has expanded inside the reception beyond.

A peacock pecks at a bed of scarlet flowers near ground-floor French windows. Daffodils. On the terrace to the south of the broad, flat facade of the great house, a figure sits alone, slumped forward in a wheelchair.

Another body lies some fifty metres distant, face-down on a neat lawn. A man, his blue dressing gown open, his thin arms thrown forward into the earth. His legs are patched with snow, his pyjamas sodden. His feet are bare and the same unhealthy blue as his hands, as if his extremities are bruised.

A distant, thick treeline beyond the gardens and empty car park on the south side of the grounds. Over there something is moving.

No sooner does a flicker of motion become evident as a moving of the foliage than the murky thing vanishes. But something pale has just loped through the trees way over there. Yes, because now there are several other forms coming. There for only a moment, darting through the spaces between the dark boughs bordering the lawns of the grounds.

The motion in the wood returns, or moves further along the forest edge and closer to the rear of the manor house before disappearing from sight. What was it? A series or cluster of white objects, even figures, between the trees that quickly passed from view. A commotion caused by no recognisable form. But the movement suggested forward momentum, like something was rushing. Can this bustle be dismissed as nothing more than rags of rubbish being dragged through the branches? But there is no wind here, nor would that account for the apparent sense of purpose, the determination and agency in those movements. Had there not also been some hint of a feline swiftness, an animal agility, in whatever has just sped across the shadowed, wooded verge before the lawns?

There it is again!

In the distance, beyond the south wing of the building, above the neat rows of flowers in the gardens, a pale object pauses on its journey before it quickly passes from sight behind the manor house. A pale shape briefly flowing until abruptly stiffening between the trees and building, creating an impression of thin legs, perhaps supporting a long upper body. The shape, or illusion, of a figure that appeared to have not been there at all. The movements made no discernible sound.

Too tall for a person, but might a fast dog cover so much ground so quickly?

The wide lawn now feels more exposed, too open to the sky where the ribbons and dregs of the fragmenting clouds saturate mauve.

From deep inside the manor house, or towards the rear, issues a sickening thump: the sound of a soft object swung or hurled against a hard surface.

Up there! The second floor! That glimpse of a body inside the room, its arms loose and swaying. But only briefly does the figure linger near the windows before it is tugged upwards, disappearing from sight.

A muffled bumping down a staircase as if an excited child were racing down to greet guests. Now there, through the wide doorway of the main entrance, the silent, unresisting figure of a lifeless elderly woman is being moved inside the hallway until she too vanishes from sight in the dim confines at the rear of the reception hall. She'd been held aloft, clear of the floor and closer to the ceiling than the ground, as if propelled by an invisible waiter who carried her flopping body upon a tray, inwards, into the dark, a silky gown cocooning her frail body.

Now there! Up above the main door. Three window-frames on the upper floor briefly display pale, moving fragments that momentarily draw together and move like heads. Might they belong to surviving residents installed in those rooms?

But then, whoever they are who are standing upright in the three unlit rooms, all of them some distance from the windows, parts of their forms are too vague or even too transparent to permit greater identification.

Gone, upwards, so fast: the elderly woman in the silky gown who was propelled through the hallway. From the far side of the house she bursts vertically, as if stepping over an edge and into the thin air surrounding a great height and a tremendous fall. She makes no sound. Up and away she goes, still falling into the sky, her gown whipping like an excited tail.

A slapping sound issues from behind, as if from a wet towel snapped through the misty air of a bathroom. Turn quickly and the figure abandoned on the thawing lawn, that casualty of a war never understood or recorded, goes up too. Cleared from the grounds and flung up, as if mere litter tossed into a deep, heaving sea: the ocean of the sky.

A rattle and chink of metal over by the manor house. Turn and see the air briefly shimmer on the patio as if the thinnest waterfall cascades over that corner. An empty wheelchair lies behind the near imperceptible distortion of the atmosphere. The wheelchair's occupant is already hundreds of metres above, falling and seemingly reaching for the ground before flopping over and plunging headfirst into the red sky.

Have the bodies here drawn something from the trees, *these trees*? So those already dead were not abandoned after all? Are they now being cleared like leftovers at a feast?

Rosy sunlight sparkles and glistens upon the eroding dunes of snow, melting to unveil flowers, the aromatic earth. The building's stucco and glass are rinsed in ruby light; its shadowy interior seems more empty than it did moments before.

A deep vermilion stains the eastern horizon and reaches west to wherever the sun is falling, being chased away. Over there, streaks of thin carmine spread like gangrene through the last of the day's natural light. Mahogany clouds cluster east, new continents of vapour patched with the colours of wet bricks. Indigo pushes behind and through the cover in all other swathes of the firmament, revealing the deep freeze of open space beyond the atmosphere. Night is coming but there is no sky, anywhere on the earth, that should look like this.

The incessant cloud cover has been breaking for hours and is now intent on melting away with the last of the snow upon the earth. But what is visible of the three-quarter moon appears too large. The visible surface of the familiar satellite is also pinked hibiscus; the outer meniscus is the rust of old meat.

And a much larger form grows in vastness without definition from behind the disintegrating rags of cloud. A mostly indistinct, jet-black shape is appearing within the outer darkness encasing the earth but is closer to the earth than the moon and not a sphere.

Part of the object, at its visible summit, becomes so dark it disappears within the encroaching night. But below the apex of the silhouette and upon this enormous, misshapen celestial body that should not be there, lumpy contours are suggested. The lower part is freckled with spots of red light, no more distinct than the moon's craters on a clear night, though these holes glimmer like rubies.

It seems suspended, poised beyond the atmosphere, though it could not be stationary; this object is either caught in the earth's orbit, or intentionally travelling at the same speed as the earth's rotation to maintain a position. Above this confusing and unfamiliar and unaccountably ruby world, what resembles a new planet is here and so dark that it strives again to become invisible in the swiftly falling night. A black immensity that has approached the earth. How long might the foreign body have travelled to get here? Perhaps it was passing the earth undetected before pausing.

Behind the manor house, a plume of smoke rises.

Story Notes:
About These Derelictions

I travelled through parts of Poland in 2006, and while in Krakow I felt I had to go and see Auschwitz. I anticipated that the experience would be humbling, upsetting and compelling in the most ghastly way. My visit was all of those things to a degree, though the experience was not as affecting as I had expected. Was I unfeeling and desensitised? Much of the horror I felt was at myself for not feeling enough, though this trip was never supposed to be about me: it was about a place that commemorated the most inhumane and horrifying behaviour that our species has proven itself able and willing and determined to enact. Perhaps this place was too much for me to properly and fully comprehend? Time would be required, time not obscured by expectation.

But the main problem, I realised, was that there were, quite simply, too many other people there at the same time. Artificiality encroached upon my visit, the atmosphere of a museum. I was also within a facsimile of a place of utmost horror and inhumanity, as almost all of the original structures and evidence was destroyed by the retreating guards. But when I later took a taxi to neighbouring Birkenau, I suddenly felt how I had expected to feel at Auschwitz. There, I felt something I'd never felt before that day and would not hurry to feel again.

Truly aghast, I became disoriented. With my silent friend, I stood in a watchtower and gazed across a landscape of barracks and other watchtowers and fences that had three tones – white, grey and black, the colour of ash. Having read so much of the horrors of the Second World War, I found myself in a place in which I felt it unwise to allow my imagination to fully extend. I could not allow it to explore those freezing wooden structures arranged in industrial rows below my feet, nor think too long about who once occupied them and how they had suffered. What had happened there was perhaps too much to consider imaginatively for very long, but it had also charged the very ground with an echo of horror. I didn't need to take a photograph; one developed indelibly in my mind.

I thought, too, about those who must have been the first to walk into other aftermaths, myriad in human history, not least the villages and churches in Rwanda half a century later, the day after the genocide burned itself out. I thought of the crime scene photographs I have viewed in the plate sections of true crime books, in documentaries and in online newspapers. One of my early horrified fascinations was a photograph of a woman's foot, lying idle beside a gas fire, a perfectly formed foot still inside a shoe beside a pile of ash. Another, in *Time Life*, of a beautiful woman who had leaped from the Empire State Building and landed on a car below. Yet another of a Japanese soldier roasted alive inside a tank, his scorched head emerging from the turret. Pure horror, single images more memorable than whole stories, books or films.

Discovering what has been left behind after an act of sheer horror is a profound experience, an idea I have always found arresting and dreadful. The discovery of such an aftermath, at a particular site or locale, would surely be framed by the sensation of a paralysis of time. Even the earth might appear to stop turning as a fuller horror is perceived. Mercifully, I only have to imagine the impact upon the senses when nothing matters but the revealed horror. But from an observer's point of view, might not such moments of complete trauma, which often occur in a place in which inhumanity or natural disasters have left wreckage, also assume an unnatural appearance and atmosphere seemingly charged by the supernormal? Because being *there* and seeing *it* is, for most of us, far beyond normal human experience.

But it is not static images of a moment that I have made the subject of this collection, but certain places and particular landscapes in which the strange and horrific are discovered. Extraordinary aftermaths are inevitably and naturally impregnated with narrative, are immediately imbued with the potential for story. To cope with the confrontation of horror, the mind fills with an appalled curiosity, with questions. How did this event or situation come about? Who were the individuals who died here? What must they have felt before the end?

Such charged spaces naturally evoke mystery, suggest presences and atmospheres, and are akin to hauntings. With hauntings, what wields most power may not be what is seen walking, or flickering briefly into animation, but the anticipation of such, or the evidence off-screen – the sound of it. And when something unnatural seems to be taking place, one also suspects that these strange infestations from a past tragedy or malfeasance could manifest themselves within that ruined castle or aged room . . . at any time.

Spaces. Places. What is left behind. Dereliction. Abandonment. Where no one is yet present, sifting, commenting, assessing, picking things up and putting them down. Where no one is yet looking, nor looking at you looking at them. This is the essence of these tales and my curiosity about empty spaces that are littered with evidence of the dreadful.

In places empty of human life, consciousness and endeavour, there remains a continuation of weather, seasons, the activity of wildlife, time. Existence doesn't halt without us present, it continues. Where human occupation has come to an end, where the thoughts of those once present have ceased, but where there is continuing *existence* with the participation of a sole consciousness (that of the reader): this was the idea that was eventually distilled into my desire to depict a particular kind of horror story.

One of the great tropes of horror stipulates that areas in which horror has occurred are thereafter charged with the 'supernormal'. Such environments challenge future inhabitants, visitants and witnesses about all they can be certain of in this life, making them confront what they wished never to confront. In these places, values, belief, certainty, the mundane, the expected and the assurances of existence continuing pretty much as it has always done . . . end. Pursuing this aesthetic goal, I have tried to create horror stories that can function without living characters; stories only requiring locations and props to tell of terrible events that have already transpired. Cold crime scenes, stage sets without actors. Though what else can be seen in the background, in the room next door, the cellar below, the bottom of a swimming pool out back?

Such tales may not require a progression of time. A progression of physical events is unnecessary because the events may have already concluded. Though not always; sometimes within the abandonment a curious process may continue to be methodically enacted. But maybe this type of weird tale, if that is what it is, can exist purely as a few moments in a particular place where no living person remains. What the tale will mean to a reader is not within my grasp to predict, but what may classify these derelictions as stories is that they are carefully plotted and all ascend to a critical mass in which an explanation of what occurred is suggested. Some narrative artifice is employed beyond mere description.

Can such a dereliction-story be dramatic, though? Will a dereliction engage a reader without clear and obvious point-of-view characters, a cast? Will a dereliction conjure mystery, even suspense? Does a dereliction even evoke the curious kind of conflict or tension required for drama to work? Will a reader care enough to walk to the end of the scene, if that is all it is: a scene? Or do these tales of absence still require a number of dramatic acts in which no one speaks, moves or does anything? That's what I wanted to find out. After all, there is so much existence and space and so many deserted places on this planet that don't contain us at all. Upon most of the surface of this earth, we're not present; we're not jabbering or doing things, or assuming significance purely by being there. But that is not to say that these places that are devoid of us lack significance, or meaning, or narrative, or horror. Naturalists and zoologists guarantee that there are an infinite number of horror stories occurring out there that not one of us is bearing witness to.

But in each of my derelictions, I did grasp the importance of *spectacle*. *Something* must *have* happened, or *still be* happening. That was another rule. If nothing had happened, if nothing continued to unfold, then it wouldn't work as fiction. Perhaps revelations of escalating power can function as the dramatic acts that combine into a story.

Though what mainly troubled me right from the start was *We* and *I. Us. You.* Characters with their first, second and third-person points-of-view. Was it possible to erase a narrator completely? I didn't manage it. Though I tried to keep narration to a murmur, an anonymous narrator with an authorial voice was still required to lead the reader through the place of dereliction. More so in some stories than in others. I couldn't help noticing that a sense of omniscience would always creep in, taking a reader into its confidence and adding a smidgen of company within environments that were depicted clinically, sterilely, dispassionately. But, despite my disappointment that narrators, or something like them, still survived, at least 'they' only served a limited purpose: to invite the reader to *take a look at this* while remaining largely alone. *What happened here is what you make of it.*

One of the great feats of horror done well is to stretch the minds of characters and the imaginations of readers into a consideration of our cosmic insignificance within vast swathes of time and space that we cannot even begin to grasp beyond formulae. But could the same effect be created without a character's point-of-view that is shared viscerally by the reader? This was the biggest obstacle to the entire venture.

What rages inside our brain-pans is almost entirely concealed from the others around us and is of little significance to them because of what rages inside their own bony cages. There are 7bn individual skulls on this planet, in a solar system more than 11bn kilometres across and a galaxy with a radius of over 52,000 light years within a universe 93bn light years wide, and our tiny life-spans, not least in relation to the age of the earth (4.5bn years) and the cosmos (13bn years), really do cease to matter much. However much we think and feel, and love ourselves, only a God could truly be aware of us intimately.

Once we're past infancy, we can't even trust others to be aware of us much, or to ascribe meaning and importance to us. That is one horror of human existence: insignificance. But it is a horror that can also be perversely liberating. I think the Buddhists grasp this. But I digress. The aesthetic aim in these stories was ultimately to demote the actions and responses and dynamism and thoughts of characters, so that only two people occupy the imaginative space: the reader and the 'thin narrator' whose task it is to guide the reader around what's just happened, by showing open doors and inviting the reader through them without saying much, or anything at all. Just the two of you go in and then come out (I hope).

But why even do it, why write the derelictions? Why put this much thought into an experiment, why invest so much time in probably the most uncommercial work of horror fiction published this year? Curiosity. The idea excited me and compelled me: two ingredients necessary for me to even begin writing anything at all. I also needed to prove another idea that I have toyed with, a notion that often comes to me when I am watching films: horror's power can exist beyond the individual and its agency and in a unique way. Set design and location and what is suggested therein, and sound, can be the most affecting things about horror on the screen.

So, in each of these derelictions, people or characters now inert were once present, but expired in what seems to have been a terrible series of frenzies enacted by supernormal or alien entities against which they had no defence, and about which they had little prior knowledge – perhaps no clue at all. Beyond the ghastly business of attempted escapes, efforts to regain control or fight back, to assert the will of man – the fundamentals of traditional characterisation – there is, to my mind, far more that can be depicted as pure horror.

There is the location, with its lingering presence of the *other*; the strangely charged atmosphere that arises from a suspension of natural law; the possibility of there being so much more than we know (enigma); imagery that seeks a connection deep within what seethes in our subconscious minds. Take *us*, or characters, out of the equation and maybe you can still have all of those facets within a horror story? I can think of a few good horror films that were spoiled by terrible characters and dialogue. Meddling goals, missions, feelings, beliefs, values, loves, fears, hopes . . . so let's just get rid of all of that for once. Remove everything but the trace elements of humanity that remain in places where lives have ended, and thus compel the reader to become voyeur.

Ultimately, the question I ask is: can fiction be interesting without human activity? Can it transport our imaginations? Can it affect? Can it, above all else, still tell a horror story? Because a story of a kind must be told. A dereliction must still be a story, or it is 'copy' and a catalogue-like description of things found somewhere; for instance, items inside a house. Can such a story of dereliction include the very substance of horror without anything much happening within it? Perhaps even nothing at all? What kind of narrative exists if it mostly travels backwards beyond the printed story and inside the reader's imagination?

I believe such a type of story can work, and well, though I might not have the skill to pull it off. It's not up to me to say these stories work and I am certain they won't please everyone; as some of you read this, others may be fighting for their keyboards to denounce the book. But, dear reader, I had to try. And at least, this may be my first book in which someone on Goodreads cannot say, 'I don't like the characters' or 'I couldn't relate to the lead character' or 'The lead character was so whiney'. But I may have spoken too soon. I am going to hazard a guess that every genre of fiction could tell a similar kind of story through an uninhabited space littered with artefacts.

I suspect that aesthetically this style of story is more filmic than literary. It may have more in common with photography and moving pictures and sculpture, or modern art installations (and I have seen some tremendous ones), than it does with the short story or novel. So I ask the reader to indulge me by treating this collection as a kind of gallery. An exhibition. Let imaginations roam the seven derelictions as if this were a movie lot in which installations had been created to hold stories filmed a long time ago . . . films that no one ever saw. There are seven installations. One will be too many for some; more than seven might be too many for others.

Anyway, a little information about the genesis of these derelictions. When I studied creative writing, many years ago, I remember an unfinished story, a work in progress, being submitted by a poet, in which no characters had been introduced; a few pages of vivid, precise description that seemed to hold a story that was only vaguely being suggested. A seed was sown. Decades later, I tinkered with a *Mary Celeste* idea, set aboard a vast container ship, in my first story of this nature, 'Hippocampus'. I half-expected the editor, Paul Finch, to say: it's not what we're looking for. He didn't. Readers liked the story too. Ellen Datlow reprinted the tale in *Year's Best Horror*. Ramsey Campbell included the story in the *Folio Book of Horror Stories*. And from this I was encouraged to continue. Maybe my crazy ship story had legs and feelers, wings and a twitching proboscis. Once the seal was broken, I couldn't help imagining new characterless stories and scenes within places where something awful had occurred. And my future derelictions could be set anywhere, as horror will happen everywhere. Horror effortlessly exists in those places where we are no longer present: it is present and continuing as a collection of artefacts, stains, residues.

In places we call home, our most familiar and comforting environments, who can say what happened in the past? We might all be sleeping above and walking across scenes of past horrors. 'My house is a new build.' For sure, but what happened on that patch of ground two thousand years ago? Don't get comfortable. And we could all be gone in a heartbeat at any time, so what any of us may leave behind, lying stiff in a bed, or slumped in an armchair, or inert upon the floor, is going to be a very real horror for someone when we're found (particularly if no one finds us for weeks).

Are these derelictions new? I honestly don't know; I've never come across one before. But, at the very least, here is a determined attempt to assemble a pure collection of them in one place. A place that lacks a roof and where a dark sky is the limit.

Manes exite paterni
Adam L. G. Nevill
South Devon
September 2019.

Acknowledgements

*T*hough Ritual Limited probably falls under the classification of self-publishing, I prefer Indie Publishing. And I'll tell you why: I cannot do it alone. Each of these books is created by a network of professionals. Manuscripts are edited and proof-read and design proof-read, text-designed, covers and cases designed, cover artwork is produced, eBooks converted, third parties distribute them and two of the UK's biggest printers print the hardbacks and paperbacks. All of it is done by other people. I write the books and project-manage the many components of the publishing critical path that ultimately delivers, I hope, a high quality edition into your hands. But it's a team not an individual who creates these books; to me it still feels like I'm working for the three publishing companies that employed me across eleven years as an editor and editorial director.

So this is the place where I can acknowledge the work and expertise of my colleagues and partners on Ritual Limited books and on *Wyrd*: Pete Marsh of The Dead Good Design Company, an experienced graphic designer and artist, who text-designs all of my books; Simon Nevill, another experienced artist, graphic designer and games designer, who designs the covers and cases of all Ritual Limited books; Samuel Araya, an artist who created the dazzling cover artwork for my last book too; Anne Nevill, my wife, who takes care of fulfilment (an arduous task involving hundreds of limited edition hardbacks), business administration, proof-reading, the website and newsletter; Tony Russell is the editor I have worked with since 2005 and Wyrd was no exception, and yet again he has made me look at my writing in a new way; Journalstone create the audio edition; TJI printed the hardback, Ingram the paperback; Brian J. Showers saves the day each time with his eagle eyes and considerable publishing experience. I recognise, acknowledge and thank them all for their contributions to this strange book.

A great many readers and reviewers then boost the signals of these books too and to each of them I extend my sincerest thanks. I am an author that has endured chiefly by word-of-mouth among readers of horror; it's been a long game but the only game I would endorse. I can't name everyone because as I write this, reviews are still flowing in, but for their kind words on *The Reddening* and other works of mine, I want to thank Sadie Hartman and Night Worms, Mindi Snyder, Tony Jones at Gingernuts of Horror, Dan Howarth at This is Horror, Pablo at The Eloquent Page, Patti at Patti's Blogspot, Marc Francis, Steel Rain Reviews, Horror Bound, Anthony Watson, Jim at Hypnogoria, Carmilla Voiez, and the many Bookstagrammers and readers who have left reviews on Goodreads and Amazon. I salute you all with both horns. Without Amazon and Ingram and Wordpress, who host my website, my horrors wouldn't reach anyone. They gave me another way to do this.

Finally, allow me to thank each and every reader who took a chance on this unusual book, in one or several of its editions. I bow in gratitude for your time, head-space and patronage.

About the Author

*A*dam L. G. Nevill was born in Birmingham, England, in 1969 and grew up in England and New Zealand. He is an author of horror fiction. Of his novels, *The Ritual, Last Days, No One Gets Out Alive* and *The Reddening* were all winners of The August Derleth Award for Best Horror Novel. He has also published three collections of short stories, with *Some Will Not Sleep* winning the British Fantasy Award for Best Collection, 2017.

Imaginarium adapted *The Ritual* and *No One Gets Out Alive* into feature films and more of his work is currently in development for the screen.

The author lives in Devon, England. More information about the author and his books is available at: www.adamlgnevill.com

Printed in Great Britain
by Amazon

966f0c00-0af6-4416-bf6f-5d89f4647169R01